I0760725

AN IMMORTALS OF INDRIELL NOVELLA

ASSIGNMENT

MELISSA A. CRAVEN

PRAISE FOR IMMORTALS OF INDRIELL

2016 RONE Award Winner – Best Book Cover
2016 YA Books Central Finalist for Best Indie
2015 Dante Rossetti YA Awards Finalist
2015 International Book Awards Finalist
2015 USA Best Book Awards Finalist

"I loved that Emerge wasn't the usual suspects, but an entirely new concept." Amazon reviewer ★★★★★

"Just when you think Allie's journey is coming to an end...Craven shows you just how wrong you were. DON'T miss the end of this book." Amazon reviewer ★★★★★

"Craven has skillfully developed a realistic Fantasy. I can almost believe this ancient race of Immortals actually lives among us." Hub Pages Reviewer ★★★★★

"Emerge is a story that begins as a single snowflake and ends in an avalanche." Amazon Reviewer ★★★★★

"Craven has a talent for keeping her reader's attention as she reveals Allie's story, layer by interesting layer." Amazon Reviewer ★★★★★

"The immortal characters in "Emerge" all have a special gift, but so does the author. Craven's is a superpower that we can all benefit from: storytelling." Amazon Reviewer ★★★★★

ASSIGNMENT: An Immortals of Indriell Novella

By: Melissa A. Craven

Midnight Hour Studio INC

Atlanta, Georgia

For more information contact: Hello@Melissaacraven.com or visit the author's website at **Melissaacraven.com**

*Previously published as Emerge: The Assignment (An Immortals of Indriell Novella) © January 24, 2018

Cover design by: Rachel Bostwick & @BooklyStyle

Edited by Rebecca Jaycox

Interior Design by @BooklyStyle

ASIN

ISBN 9798695511642 paperback

First edition for print October 22, 2020

Printed in the United States of America

A FREE OFFER!

In Assignment, find out what happens when Tessa St. James receives her first Assignment as a Soma Agent. And then download your FREE copy of SCHOLAR and discover everything there is to know about the Immortals of Indriell.

Visit http://bit.ly/SCHOLARoffer to download now!

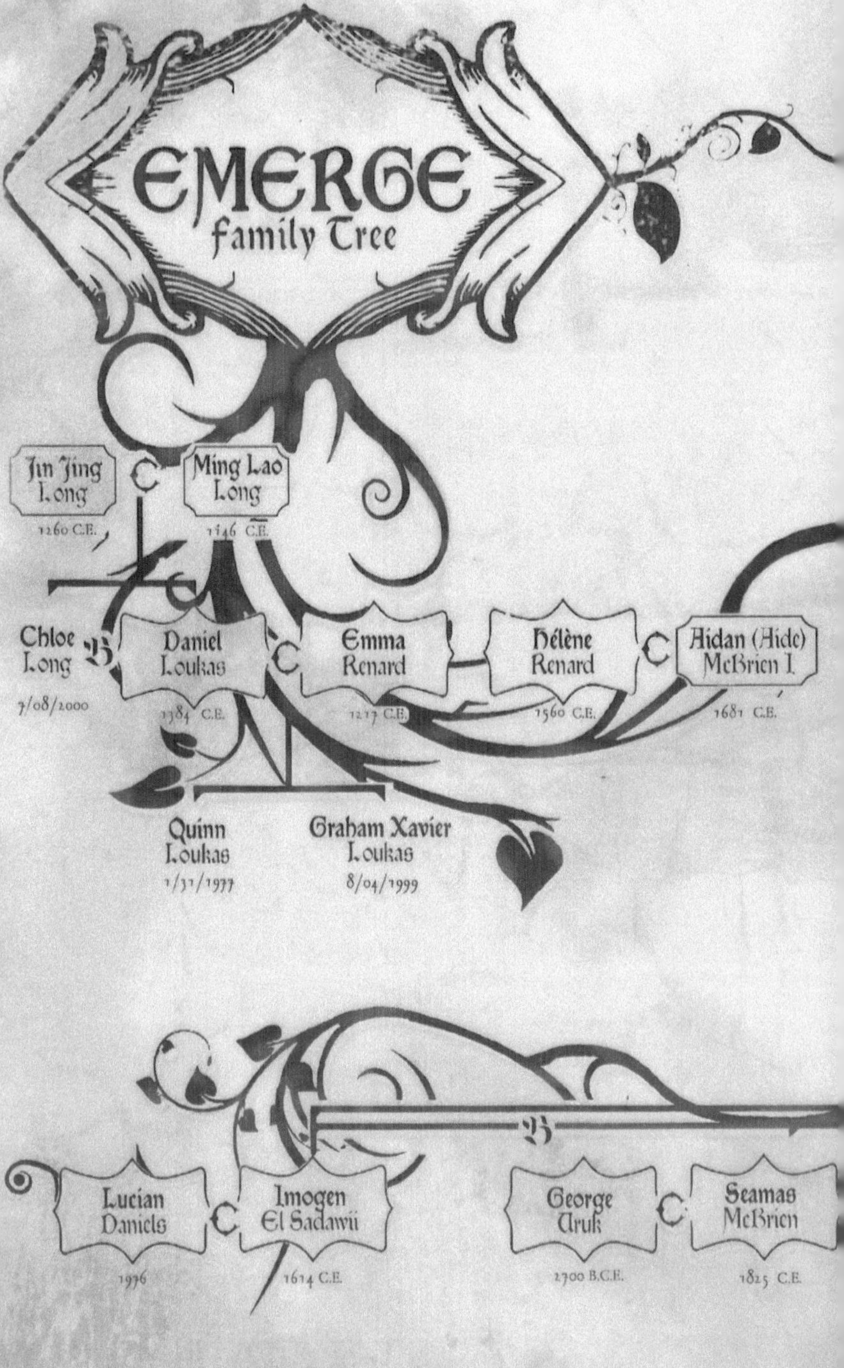

EMERGE
Family Tree
Jin Jing Long
1260 C.E.
C
Ming Lao Long
1146 C.E.
Chloe Long
7/08/2000
B
Daniel Loukas
1384 C.E.
C
Emma Renard
1217 C.E.
Hélène Renard
1560 C.E.
C
Aidan (Aide) McBrien I.
1681 C.E.
Quinn Loukas
1/31/1977
Graham Xavier Loukas
8/04/1999
B
Lucian Daniels
1976
C
Imogen El Sadawii
1614 C.E.
George Uruk
2700 B.C.E.
C
Seamas McBrien
1825 C.E.

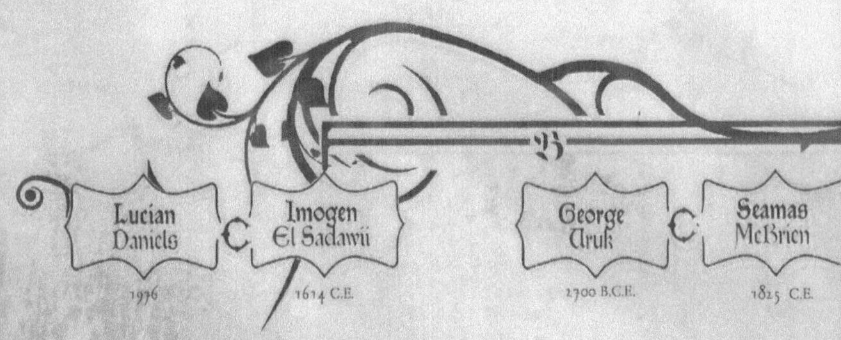

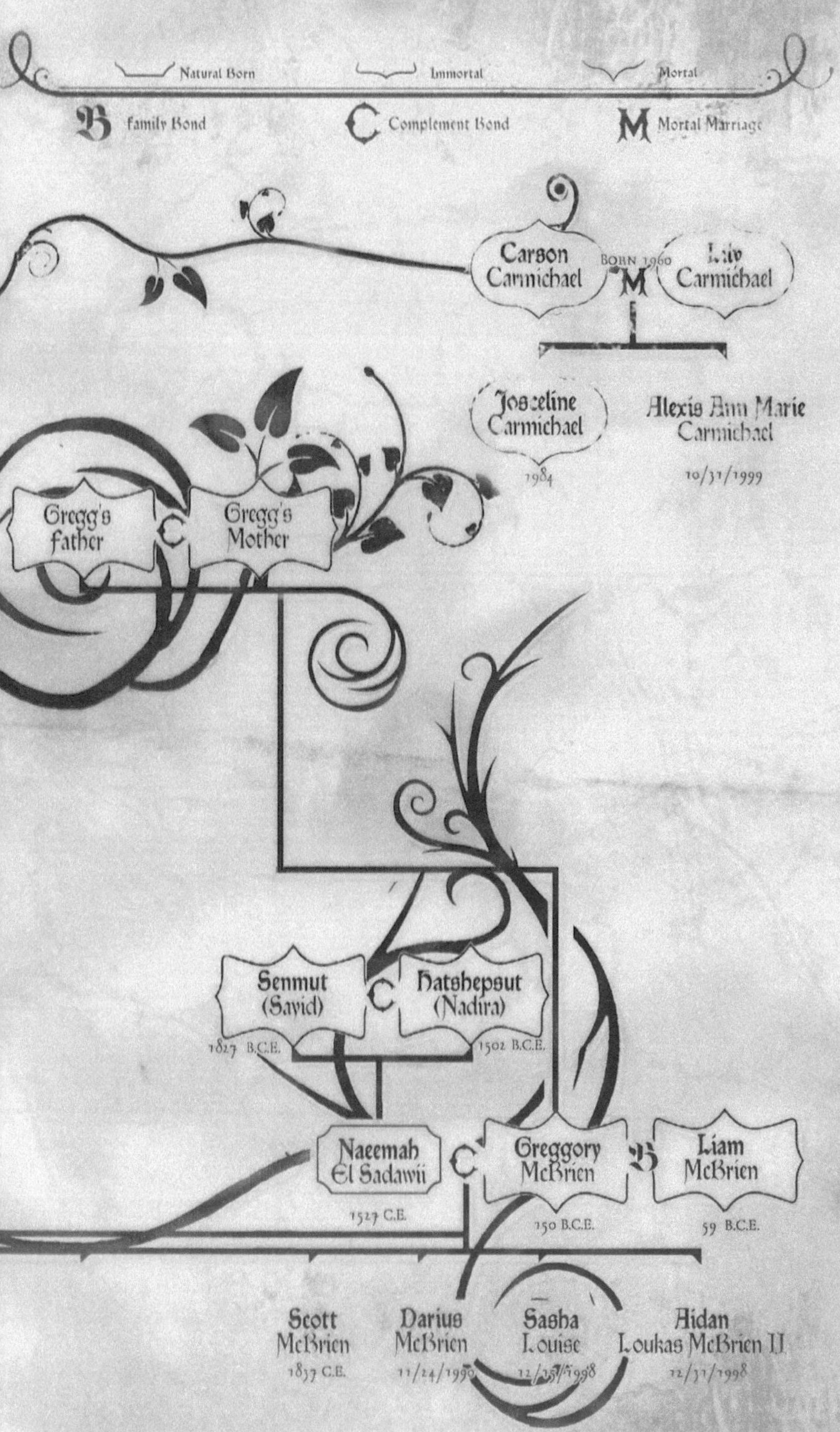
Natural Born
Immortal
Mortal
B family Bond
C Complement Bond
M Mortal Marriage
Carson Carmichael
BORN 1960
M
Liv Carmichael
Josceline Carmichael
1984
Alexis Ann Marie Carmichael
10/31/1999
Gregg's father
C
Gregg's Mother
Senmut (Sayid)
1827 B.C.E.
C
Hatshepsut (Nadira)
1502 B.C.E.
Naeemah El Sadawii
1527 C.E.
C
Greggory McBrien
150 B.C.E.
B
Liam McBrien
59 B.C.E.
Scott McBrien
1837 C.E.
Darius McBrien
11/24/1990
Sasha Louise
12/25/1998
Aidan Loukas McBrien II
12/31/1998

CHAPTER 1

"And our champion is ... the little blond weighing in at barely a hundred pounds," Ben announced to the thunderous applause echoing along the crumbling old subway tunnel.

With the strength of a dozen Immortals coursing through her veins, Tessa glared daggers at him. Every time she won Amrita, Ben had something snarky to say about her size. Sure, she was petite, but with her gift, Tessa could overpower just about anyone in the right circumstances-and Amrita provided just that. Even now after fighting in the melee all evening, Tessa rode a high only a true fight in front of a crowd could give her. She was the strongest person in the arena tonight. She was the strongest person in any arena most nights. Her power fed off of the crowd's excitement and the force of the other fighters. If Ben knew what was good for him, he'd shut the hell up.

"Nice job as usual, sweetheart." Ben held her hand up, and the crowd roared its approval. But Tessa was busy calculating how much cash she would be adding to her Soma account. The purse was fifty-thousand dollars, but she never saw the whole take. She usually walked away with less than half after she split her winnings with Soma, and tipped the staff their customary twenty percent.

When she signed on to work the Amrita circuit, Livia, the head of Soma, demanded she sign a minimum of a five year contract. Tessa had big plans for her future, and it didn't include working the circuit longer than necessary. In exchange for a shorter contract, Tess had agreed to return half of her winnings to Soma each month, effectively buying out her five year contract two years early. This was her last year, and it was almost over. She could see the finish line. She'd managed just fine on her take of the winnings for the last three years. But precious little was left over after she reimbursed Soma for her college tuition, her personal trainers, and sent what she could home to her mother. There were other expenses associated with being an elite member of the Soma training and education program. A small price to pay to ensure a brilliant future for a girl who had no interest in working two jobs just to get by like her single mother had.

"Don't forget to see me before you leave," Ben reminded her.

"Don't worry; you'll get your money."

Ben was on the take wherever he could make a buck. She wasn't sure how much of the twenty percent the rest of his staff saw, but it was worth every penny to keep him happy and off her back.

Tessa wandered through the crowd and like always, she dreaded the long evening ahead. The fighting part she was born for, but the social game of Amrita was just not something she excelled at. After a night in the arena limelight, she fully intended to take up her natural place among the wallflowers, hunker down, and wait for dawn.

I'd rather be home binge watching Hulu in my bathrobe with a pint of mint chocolate chip ice cream and some peace and quiet.

"Brilliant fight," an admirer called as Tess headed for the bar. She smiled and waved at all the well wishers. Some of them were frequent Amrita guests. If they knew this whole thing was rigged for their entertainment they'd be crushed. The fights were real enough, but the winner of Amrita was always on staff, and thanks to Ben's gift, the regulars never realized they'd seen her win before.

Amrita was a business. It was a fun atmosphere and gave the younger generations a place to blow off steam. It could also be dangerous, so Tess liked to fly under the radar as much as possible. But she wasn't completely naive. She knew the real point of Amrita was to lure in the best and brightest of her generation-and the wealthiest. It was a recruiting pool for Soma. Those lucky enough to be chosen tonight would receive the best education an Immortal could hope for. But her job was done for the night. She'd leave the recruiting to people like James who were better suited to schmoozing and socializing.

"Newcastle, please?" Tess nodded at the bartender busy serving fancy cocktails to those uninterested in the champagne fountains.

Training and working at Soma was difficult, but her mother had moved mountains for her to be there. Tessa had a wonderful childhood with her single mom, but Susan St. James just didn't have the resources or the time to invest in her daughter's training. So at the age of eight, Susan enrolled Tessa into the Fold-a subset of Soma for younger children-hoping they could offer her daughter the kind of life she never had. Susan had sacrificed everything for her daughter and Tess would be forever grateful for the opportunities her mother had worked so hard to provide. And some day soon, she would be the one taking care of her mother.

Those first few years at the Fold were like day camp. But as she grew older, Tessa spent more and more time with her trainers and less time with her mother, until she finally moved into the student dorms at Sterling Tower. In the years leading up to her Awakening, Tessa worked hard to make her mother proud, moving up in the ranks of her class. Only a few elite students of the Fold earned the honor of continuing their education with Soma, and after her Awakening, Tessa was one of them. She gladly took on her own tuition payments to relieve her mom of the financial burden.

She was so proud the day Livia herself invited Tessa to continue her studies at Sterling Tower.

"This is your home, Tess," Livia had said. "For as long as you want to stay with us."

Livia promised her a bright a future if she continued to perform as well as she had for the Fold. Already, at nineteen, Tessa was a top tier student and got to travel the globe on private jets, staying in the best hotels each month as she worked the Amrita circuit. The rest of the month, she lived in a posh apartment in Atlanta's Midtown and trained with world-class Soma agents. She waited anxiously for the day she would receive her first assignment and become a Soma agent herself. She would do important work for the Immortal world. And when she was able, she and her mother would get to know each other again. The distance and the years had made them strangers, but in Tessa's mind it was all part of the sacrifice to build a better future for both of them. For now, Tessa felt good about sending her mother a small stipend every month.

"You look like you hate this as much as I do." A deep voice brought her out of her thoughts.

Tessa eyed the Immortal sliding into the seat beside her. The same old nerves clenching her gut. She hated small talk. Only because she was so bad at it. "You were first up?" She recognized the handsome guy as the first to fight tonight. He'd won his round and had a hell of a good time doing it, but failed to make it to the final melee.

"You were amazing." His vivid, white smile shone brightly against his ebony skin.

Tessa caught herself wondering what her ivory skin would look like beside his, but quickly discarded the thought. As lonely as she was, she just didn't have time for relationships and flirtations. She'd make time for frivolous things like that once she had her first assignments behind her.

"Thanks." She returned his smile but shifted her eyes back to the half-peeled label of her beer bottle.

"You won a huge prize, so why do you look so miserable?"

"I love the fights, but I'd rather skip the party," she admitted with a tentative smile. It really wasn't worth the massive anxiety socializing put her through. He'd be gone in a few hours, and she'd be on a private jet back to Atlanta by morning, after a blissfully quiet night in her suite at the Ritz Carleton. But she found herself turning toward him despite her reservations.

"Can we get a couple of beers here?" he asked the bartender. "I hate champagne."

"Me too," Tess said. "Makes me dizzy."

"Brave move." He tapped his bottle against her fresh Newcastle.

"What, winning?" She shot him a confused look.

"Showing this crowd how your gift works. I can't decide if it was brave or really stupid." He took a sip of his beer.

"Well, thanks for the drink." She slid off her stool to leave. *And thanks for reminding me why I don't flirt.*

"Wait, no." He grabbed her wrist to halt her retreat. "That came out really wrong. I'm an idiot like that. That was supposed to be a compliment. It's brave of you to show your gift off like that, but I'm guessing you have a whole lot more in your arsenal that we haven't seen tonight."

"Maybe." Tess cast a glance up at him before she returned to her seat. "And maybe I am just that stupid." She smiled.

"Where's everyone going?" He nodded at the crowd surging toward the train station lobby and away from the arena.

"The after party," Tess said, watching how quickly the arena bar was emptying. The train lobby had been transformed into a posh nightclub and the crowd was eager for the night ahead. "I guess it's time to celebrate my big win." This was the part Tess hated the most about her Amrita duties. The party. The aura wafting in from the dance floor was already pulling at her. She knew better than to ignore it. "Coming?" Tess held her hand out for him-her inhibitions slipping away.

"If I must." He slid off the bar stool and wrapped his hand around hers. She marveled at the way their skin glowed against each other's. Warmth tingled in her fingertips at his touch. She couldn't remember the last time she'd held someone's hand.

Am I really nineteen years old and holding a boy's hand for the first time?

She couldn't handle how pathetic that was.

"Isn't there like a lounge for the quiet people? The introverts who'd literally rather do anything else?"

"A room filled with puppies where people don't make eye contact or chit chat, but play with the dogs instead." She laughed. It was unusual meeting someone who seemed to hate socializing even more than she did.

"Yes, where's that room? I want to go there." He smiled down at her.

"Unfortunately, I think we have to go act like extroverts now." The atmosphere whirled around them like an intoxicating fog. It relaxed her and opened her mind to the idea of spending a flirty night with a cute boy.

"But ... I've been doing that all night."

"Suck it up tough guy." She tugged him toward the crowd moving along the tunnel. "Feel the pull?"

"Yeah. This fog stuff is making me brave." He leaned in, wrapping his arm around her waist. "Call me Dean." His lips brushed against her ear, sending a shiver down her body. "Dance with me?"

"I thought you hated parties." She turned to face him.

"With a fiery passion, but I love to dance. It doesn't require talking." He backed onto the dance floor, pulling her along with him.

The smoke and lights made the other dancers fade into the background. The bump of the bass and the rhythm of the music matched her heartbeat as they began to move together.

In all of her time at Amrita, she'd never fully appreciated the experience. She tended to resist the intoxicating lure and allowed herself to enjoy watching from the sidelines, but she'd never truly participated before. Tonight, it was like the party was a living, breathing thing, and it could sense her mood, understanding that she and Dean didn't want to be overwhelmed by the crowd. In the midst of a roaring dance club, they were alone, and Tessa's hesitations were gone.

"How is this possible?" She gave into the euphoria of the moment. With Dean's arms around her, swaying to the sultry beat of the music, she felt at home. Relaxed.

"What?" Dean smiled down at her.

"Is there really a man who gets me?" she blurted.

"Do I?" he teased. "What's your preference. Library or concert?"

"Uh, library for sure," Tess replied. "Vegas or the beach?" she countered.

"The beach and a set of headphones, no contest. Partying at the Super Bowl with strangers or a night home with your two best friends?"

"Friends," Tess said softly. But she didn't really know what that was like either. She didn't have any close friends.

"I didn't want to come tonight, but my sister dragged me here. Good thing she's annoyingly persistent." Dean nodded toward a quiet alcove under a set of arches and maneuvered them across the dance floor. "I would have missed out on this. A beautiful girl just as socially awkward as me."

"I don't know; you're pretty good at this. You came on to me, remember?"

"I'm pretty sure I also accidentally insulted you when I was trying to flirt."

"You made a smooth recovery."

"Sitting alone at the bar, you looked just like I felt. I couldn't let that opportunity go."

"Am I that easy to read?" Tessa sat on a stone bench along the sidelines. Close enough to feel like a part of the party, but far enough to keep them in their own little world.

"Not even a little bit." His arm slid around her as he joined her on the bench. "I'm still trying to figure you out. Everyone else is here for a fun night out with friends. A break from the monotony of training."

"And me? What am I here for?" she asked.

His beautiful smile lit his face. "You? You're here for me."

CHAPTER 2

"Do we need to have a vocabulary lesson?" Tessa rolled her eyes at Dean. "Do you not understand the meaning of anonymous?"

Dean shrugged. "Doesn't apply."

She laughed at his wide-eyed, innocent look. Spending the evening with Dean had turned out to be one of the best nights she'd had in a long time. Certainly the most fun she'd ever had at Amrita.

"What? Am I exempt from the rules?"

"I trust you. Even if you won't tell me your real name."

"How do you know Tabitha isn't my real name?" She shifted back on the bench, giving him her best fake smile.

"You look nothing like a Tabitha."

Tessa almost jumped out of her skin when his warm hand met the bare flesh at her back, just between the hem of her shirt and the waist of her jeans. The shock of such intimacy told her she'd spent far too long without normal human contact.

"What do I look like?" she murmured shyly, her breath catching in her throat at the look in his eye.

"Something I want to devour," he whispered as his lips met hers.

The kiss was slow and languid at first, catching her completely unaware. The insanity of the moment sent off all of Tessa's warning bells. She should never get this close to anyone at Amrita but Dean was different. She should be feeling clumsy and terrified, but in his arms, she was only eager for the kiss to continue. Everything about this night was so strange. She knew she should walk away now, but in that moment, Tess wanted nothing more than to spend a fun and flirty night kissing Dean. She could walk away a happy woman after that.

"Don't stop," she whispered when he drew back.

His eyes blazed with the dim light of his power as a low growl escaped his lips. His mouth crushed against hers, the desperate longing to connect lingering between them. They were the same. That's what made him so compelling. She could feel it in her bones. Dean understood her.

Tessa arched against him, her hands running up his chest and around his neck.

His kisses trailed down to her jaw and along the column of her throat. She titled her head back to give him better access, a blissful moan on her lips.

They'd claimed the alcove for themselves, but other couples came and went among the shadows, reminding them they were not alone. But the steady thump of the music and pulse of the lights felt like it belonged just to them.

"I could totally be a Tabitha." Tessa finally pulled away to catch her breath.

"I call bullshit." Dean laughed. "But you don't have to give me your real name. It doesn't matter. I'll just call you Steve." He twined his fingers with hers.

"Don't you dare. But why did you tell me yours?" She frowned, grasping his hand with both of hers. "It's not a smart thing to do in a place like this for a powerful guy like you." It was never a good idea to put your power out on display for the world to see. That was what made Amrita so dangerous. It was difficult not to show all your cards in a game like this. Tessa was lucky enough to have one gift that enabled her to get through the night as the winner. Her remaining gifts, she'd kept close to the belt. Others weren't so lucky and had to rely on their entire arsenal of abilities to make it to the final melee.

"I'm not all that powerful."

"You must surround yourself with some pretty impressive Immortals if you think that is remotely true." She could feel his power as strongly as her own.

"I have some powerful friends." He nodded across the room to the hellacious redhead and her dark, broody dance partner.

"They should have won this whole thing," Tess murmured, wondering why two such insanely powerful people would hold back when they could have easily taken the purse for themselves. She wasn't sure how much her gift would have really helped her against either of them. Against the pair of them, she'd have no chance at all.

"We're not here for entertainment," Dean said. "It's best if we not call too much attention to ourselves."

"Please, I don't want to know why you guys are here. Don't tell me any more." Dean was far too free with information about himself and his friends.

"You're trustworthy," he said simply.

"You're naive."

"Not naive. I have a quirky little gift that tells me when a person is honest. A little something I inherited from my grandmother. My gift tells me you're one of the most honest and loyal people I've ever met."

"You shouldn't talk about your gifts. Not here." Tess darted a look around them.

"What are you so afraid of?" Dean said softly.

"Amrita isn't just a game," she hissed. She shouldn't tell him any more. Soma would want to recruit those just like him and his friends. Part of her wanted to let that happen, so she wouldn't have to let him go at the end of the night, but another part of her knew that the life she'd chosen for herself was not for everyone.

"Like I said, we're not here for a fun distraction, Tabitha.

We have a very good reason to be here, looking for clues about our missing friend."

"TMI, Dean." Tess shivered. She didn't want to know the details about them or their missing friend.

"He's actually my uncle, and he means a great deal to my cousin over there." He pointed at a beautiful, tall young woman with golden brown skin. She wasn't as inconspicuous as her friends were. She looked like she was grilling one of the Amrita guards about his mark. Tess shifted uncomfortably to make sure her own mark on her ankle was covered.

"She'll stop at nothing to get him back," Dean said softly. "Amrita's a place where you can find information if you look carefully enough and talk to the right people. So we're here for him."

"She's going to call too much attention to you guys."

"You know an awful lot about what goes on here."

"Anonymity, Dean." She shrugged, refusing to tell him about her connection with the club. "If you're here for your uncle, then why are you spending so much time talking to me?"

"You are an unexpected distraction."

"You get distracted easily." She glanced nervously down at her hands in his. "Can't you feel it?" Dean whispered, reaching to cup her face.

"What?"

"The connection between us? It's been an instant reaction for both of us. I took one look at you at the bar and couldn't walk away."

"What the hell are you talking about?" Her voice cracked, and she licked her lips nervously.

"Relax." Dean chuckled at the look of horror on her face. "I'm not saying you're my Complement; I've just never met an equal before. I imagine this is how it feels, though." He brushed his thumb across her bottom lip, tilting her face up to meet his gaze. "Instant comfort with another human being, who happens to be a lot like me in some ways and opposite in others. I don't know about you, but that's not something I experience every day."

"Equals?" Tess murmured. That would explain her strong reaction to Dean. And the growing dread of what it would do to her to walk away from him.

"We are simpatico. I've seen it before." He nodded again at the redhead and the handsome boy who never left her side. "It's a powerful thing when two equals meet. I'm not this smooth guy." A frown creased his forehead. "I have no game. Ever. But my awkward game is epic."

"I find that hard to believe," Tessa said. He'd said and done all the right things, all night.

"It's you. You make me comfortable in my own skin," he insisted. Tessa had to admit, he made her feel the same way. "Equals." The word sounded strange on her lips. It wasn't a rare occurrence. It happened often in the modern world where meeting other Immortals wasn't as difficult as it used to be. But it wasn't something that typically happened at their age. "I think you're right." She squeezed his hand. It would be that much harder to let him go now that she knew what drew them together.

"But?" Dean arched a brow at her.

"It can't come to anything."

"We can be friends," Dean said. "Amrita is an anonymous place for a reason, but this is something special. I don't want to leave tonight knowing I'll never see you again."

"Neither do I, but it has to be that way, Dean. I'm sorry." What would it mean to have a real friend in her life? Dean was someone she could easily fall for. But she couldn't afford that kind of distraction. Could she? And could he ever understand her ties to Soma? Her ambition?

A smile tugged at the corners of her mouth as she thought just maybe he might get it. Then her smile wilted at the sight of Ben making his way through the crowd.

"You need to go." Tess shot to her feet, pulling Dean up behind her. "Just for a second. I'll come find you at the bar." She nudged his shoulder.

"What's wrong?" He glanced up at Ben's approaching figure.

"Nothing. I'm right behind you. Promise."

Dean nodded and turned to melt into the crowd.

"Made a friend tonight?" Ben asked. "That's a first. I've never seen you actually enjoy these parties. It's about time you loosened up."

"It's nothing. What did you need? I've left your tip with your assistant like always." Tessa crossed her arms as if to protect herself from Ben. He was a jerk, but he was also her boss.

"Recruit your friend," Ben said. "And more importantly, his friends. He arrived with two girls, but they joined with the redhead and her boyfriends. We need to bring them all in. They are exactly what we are looking for tonight."

Tessa shook her head in confusion. "I've never been trained to recruit."

"But you have an in with your boy. He trusts you. Recruit him and the others, and you'll get to keep all of your winnings tonight." Ben turned and walked away, leaving her gaping at him.

The temptation was there. She needed the money. Living and training at Soma was so expensive. Having her full winnings would finally put her ahead.

An unexpected surge of anxiety filled her. It wasn't even a question. She'd chosen her life at Soma because it was right for her, but it wasn't a life she would wish for Dean—not at his age. Growing up in the Fold had prepared her for the demands of Soma. There was no way she was recruiting him tonight. She had to get Dean and his friends out of here.

"I need your help," Tessa said to the stocky young man at the edge of the dance floor. James was the closest thing she had to a friend at Soma. They shared some of the same secrets and counted on each other when an ally was needed.

"A reoccurring theme tonight," James said with a knowing smile. "What's up little Tessie?"

"Must you?" She rolled her eyes at the childhood nickname.

"I must. Now, what have you gotten yourself into? I saw you with Mr. Brown eyes over there. You looked cozy."

"Ben wants me to recruit him." She let a little of the panic she was feeling into her voice. "What do I do? I don't want ... I can't let that happen."

"I've always told you not to get too close."

"I got too close. Now, I need to make him and his friends disappear."

"Use your rank."

"My rank?" She was a class four student with trainer status. About as high as you could go as a Soma student.

"Girl, are you blind?" James sighed patiently. "You have a rank for a reason. Half of the Amrita employees think of you as a celebrity, and the other half is afraid of you. Use that to your advantage."

"How?"

"Walk out of here like you own the place. I'll keep Ben occupied while you do whatever it is you need to do."

"There you are." Dean's smile did something to light her up inside. It wasn't just the male attention, although she'd had precious little of that in her nineteen years. It was just him and knowing without a doubt in her mind that he was right. They were equals. Everything in her responded to him and reminded her of how lonely she in with her solitary life. She couldn't face letting him go before they had a chance to explore this thing between them, but they were out of time. Dean needed to leave before he discovered more about Amrita than he ever wanted to know.

Tessa had always supported Soma and their agenda to reach the younger generations to ensure they were properly trained. So many families insisted on sticking to the old ways. Keeping their kids at home and teaching them the way they'd been taught hundreds and even thousands of years ago. It was more important than ever for her generation to break away from the traditionalists to be taught by those who actually understood their modern gifts. Soma was the teacher so many of them needed, but it was a hard life. She didn't feel right about coercing anyone into it. Amrita existed because Soma needed new students. Most of those who came to Soma understood what they were getting into, and how lucky they were to be accepted. Dean was not one of those students. He was obviously trained well and didn't need Soma. And there was a big part of Tessa that just didn't want to see him make the kind of sacrifices she had.

"It's time for you and your friends to leave," she said quietly as she joined him at the bar. "Now."

"What's going on?" Dean asked, glancing around the bar with a worried frown.

"No questions. Just trust me, okay?"

"Okay." He nodded. "We have what we came for now." His hands tightened into fists at his sides. "We're going to get Quinn back."

"Quinn?" Tessa gasped. It couldn't be the same Quinn. She'd seen him around Soma often these last months. But she saw the family resemblance in Dean's strong jaw and lean build. He looked a great deal like his uncle. Not that she knew all that much about Livia's star pupil. What on earth could Dean and his friends have learned about Quinn tonight? He was back at Sterling Tower, far away from anything to do with Amrita. This was the last place Dean and his friends needed to be poking around for clues about their friend. Like it or not, Quinn was with Soma now. They needed to let him go and respect his decision to train with Livia. She and a million others would give anything to have that chance.

Dean scowled down at her, his jaw ticking with tension, but he let the subject drop. "You're right. It's time we left."

"Can you get a message to all of them quickly? Tell them to follow us at a discrete distance?"

Dean nodded. "Be right back."

She watched as he made his way through the crowd, seemingly comfortable with the party scene, like he was having the time of his life. He spoke with the redhead and returned to Tessa's side at the bar.

"Are we good?" she asked.

"Let's go." Dean chugged the last of his beer and took her hand casually, but the warmth and easiness between them was gone now. As if speaking about Quinn had broken the spell of their romantic night together.

Tess walked slowly with Dean at her side, trying to come up with a plan. One by one, his friends joined them seamlessly. They were so ... natural together. Tessa's heart was pounding out of her chest, yet they all acted like a group of popular kids at the prom.

"What's our next move?" Dean asked, twining his fingers with hers. "You've got this. Just tell us what we need to do." He gave her hand a gentle squeeze, but he still seemed miles away from her now.

"Follow me." Tessa took a deep breath, dropping his hand and taking the lead. "Stay close. We're only going to get one shot at this." She headed back down the corridor toward the VIP room with Dean and his friends at her back.

A few guests lingered at the buffet as the crowd thinned near the arena. The euphoria of the last hours left her as they retreated across the quiet space.

"What's up Natalie, er ... wait, it's Tabitha, right?" The Amrita guard was just the guy she wanted to see. He was new and dumber than a box of dirt.

"Heya, Tim." She gave him a brilliant smile. "Just taking these guys to visit Ben." She pointed over her shoulder at Dean and his ridiculously large group of friends. They were all idiots for coming here together like this. Individually, they might have pulled it off, but together they were bound to draw unwanted attention.

How did I get caught up in this mess? Right, the cute boy

at the bar. She caught Dean's gaze and gave him a hesitant smile. He returned her smile, but she got the sense he no longer trusted her. That crushed something inside her.

"Oh, good, Ben's expecting you," Tim said. He was busy stacking up all the rock climbing gear from each of the arrival points along the subway tunnel.

Tessa had arrived by limo, but all of the Amrita guests had to prove their worth by scaling the enormous Detroit Avenue bridge to gain access to the arena. Neat piles of cam clips, bundled in groups of five, lay in precise lines across the table. Boxes of ropes and safety gear the guests weren't offered were already packed and ready to go beside the table. Those were for the Amrita staff's use during set up and take down, which meant take down was complete, and no one would notice a few kids scaling the bridge now.

"He's in his office on the west bank." Tim pointed down the long, dark tunnel. "You can't miss it. It's the only way out."

"Thanks, I've been looking for him everywhere." Tessa shot him a grateful smile as she quickly grabbed two sets of cam clips when he wasn't looking. "Come with me, guys." She waved for her "recruits" to follow.

Tessa set an authoritative pace along the train tracks, daring anyone to ask her what she was up to. Dean and his curly haired cousin tailed her closely while the others dropped back a few paces. She wasn't even sure they really understood what was happening right now, but if Tess was caught helping them slip away, they'd all be in a boatload of trouble. She'd probably get kicked out of Soma for it.

"We have to move fast," she whispered.

"We won't get far with those few clips you swiped."

"It might be enough for you all to make it to the street above us, though." She grabbed his hand and moved quickly out of Tim's sight. "Through here," she muttered, ducking through the narrow arches that stood between them and the open night. The wind whipped Tessa's hair as she leaned over the side of the bridge to see if they had a shot of making it to the top. "Right there." She pointed to the nearest concrete pilaster. "You can climb up." She pressed the clips into Dean's hand.

"I've got it," the cousin said, taking the cams and climbing out the archway like she did this kind of thing every day. "Send the others up behind me." She leaned back in a moment later after placing the first of the cam clips into the solid concrete wall.

One by one, Dean's friends filed out of the arched opening, moving swiftly and quietly.

"Thanks," the redhead said, dipping her head back inside after climbing out. "I like her." She nodded at Dean. "She's good people."

"I'll be right behind you," Dean said, turning back toward Tess. "Look, I—"

Tessa grabbed his shoulders and pulled him down to meet her frantic kiss. His mouth pressed firmly against hers, and they leaned into each other. Their painful parting was only a breath away.

"Come with us." Dean pressed his forehead against hers, pulling her toward the edge.

"Part of me wants to, but I just ... I can't." She pulled her hand from his vise grip. "You have to go, Dean." She shoved him through the archway.

He cupped her face, pressing his lips to hers one last time, and then he was gone.

"My name is Tessa," she called into the darkness behind him.

Chapter 3

"What do you mean they left?" Ben stood behind his temporary desk, towering over Tess like an ominous storm cloud.

"I looked for them all night." Tess tried to put the right amount of earnest sincerity in her voice, but she wasn't a good liar. She was quite terrible at it, actually. "I'm not a recruiter, Ben. I haven't had that kind of training. You know I'm a top tier student. Recruiting has never been part of my curriculum."

"You spent all night with the brown one."

"The *brown* one, really? Do you even hear yourself right now?"

"In Egypt, I was an original brown one. I get to say that. Now, tell me how he slipped away like a ghost. One minute he was with you and the next, they all disappeared."

"I tried to tell him about Soma but I spooked him. He

and his friends are crazy powerful. Who knows what they did after I ran him off?"

"You actually used the name Soma? Are you stupid? Remind me never to use you for recruiting ever again."

"Relax. In three months, I'll be out of your hair forever."

"You've been counting the days since you started working my club. You think you're better than this place."

"Quite frankly, yes, I am. My assignment is coming through soon. Livia promised."

"That was before her new prized pupils joined her household. Liv's forgotten all about you with Santi and Quinn at her heels like well-trained puppies."

"Not so well-trained from what I hear," Tess muttered. "Can I go now? I have a suite at the Ritz calling my name."

"Go." Ben pointed at the door. "Just don't ever screw up like that again on my watch."

"Then don't ask me to do something that's not in my job description." Tess held her head high as she exited Ben's makeshift office at the west end of the Detroit Avenue Bridge. Her limo waited there to take her back to her hotel. With shaky hands, she slid into her seat and smiled as the driver closed the door behind her. Alone at last, Tessa's whole body began to shake with the severity of what she'd done.

I've never defied Soma before. In all her years as a student, she'd always done whatever was asked of her. Always eager to please, she towed the line and never gave anyone trouble. She could have been expelled for what she just did. And she'd risk it all over again for another night with Dean.

Tessa rested her head against the leather seat, taking a deep breath as the driver took her back across the bridge to her hotel downtown. She scoured the night for a glimpse of Dean, but there was no trace of the boy who claimed he was her equal.

She brushed her fingertips across her lips, trying to hold on to the memory of his kiss.

You have to forget him, Tess. Equal or not, there was no room for Dean in the life she'd built for herself.

"Tessa! It's good to have you back," Chase called as she made her way down the long white corridors of Sterling Tower, her suitcase rolling along behind her. Coming home was always a relief to Tessa, but this time she was returning a little bit heartbroken over what might have been. Talking to her trainer was not on her list of things she wanted to do tonight.

"I'm glad I caught you." He stood between her and the door to her apartment. "We have to step up your training for the rest of the year. You've got some progress to make before you meet with Livia in December for your yearly review. That gives us a little more than three weeks before you're leaving for Amrita again at the end of the month. Let's meet at five tomorrow morning and again on Thursday to get a jump on it before November starts slipping away from us."

"That's double my regular training hours." A stab of panic shot through Tessa at the thought of what it would cost for so much extra time with Chase. He was the best Soma had to offer, and her time with him was worth every penny. But he was also the most expensive and sought after trainer in Sterling Tower.

"Come on, Tess. You just came home with a huge Amrita purse. The 'I can't afford it' excuse doesn't work when you're pulling in the kind of money you are every month."

"You do know I don't get all of the purse, right? I don't even get half of it."

"That's still a lot of money for a nineteen year old. Don't you have a financial advisor? I hope you aren't spending your money on frivolous things. I'd hate to see you unable to afford your time with me. It's so important as close as you are to becoming a full agent."

"I'll be there," Tess promised. She would figure out the finances later. Thankfully, Soma covered most of her living expenses, so she could cut some corners to come up with the extra cash. Soma would float her a loan if she really needed it.

"How were my last samples?" she asked.

"Not bad but still not pure yet. We're almost there, Tess. And then I'll feel confident enough to recommend you for your first assignment."

"Thank you, Chase. I know I couldn't do it without you."

"Bright and early tomorrow?" He squeezed her shoulder.

"See you there," she promised. She'd give him the moon if he'd just get out of her way, so she could get into her apartment. Only a few special students got to live in the apartments at Sterling Tower, rent free. The luxury space was just one of the many perks she enjoyed, but it was by far her favorite. Most of the other students lived in the dormitories. Tess had hated her time in the dorms. It was torture with so many screaming tweens swarming the small spaces with the walls pressing in on her, and never having a single second alone.

Tess dropped her bags in the white marble foyer, the echo sounding through her silent apartment. Her cleaning lady would see to it her clothes were washed and put away.

Her cell beeped with a call from the front desk.

"Welcome back, Ms. St. James," Eric said as soon as she answered. "Can we get anything for you this evening?"

"Knock it off with the professional bullshit, Eric." He was a riot, and she loved having him as her personal concierge. But he didn't understand personal space at all-nor her desire for alone time.

"You want pizza again, don't you?"

"Yes, please. Order from that place I like." She tapped her fingernail on the cool granite surface of the kitchen counter. It felt good to be home, but at the same time, she suddenly felt lonely.

"You want your regular grocery order for the week, too?

"Just don't sneak brussel sprouts into my veggie order again. Like, ever again." Tessa paced across her apartment to the living room.

"You'd like them, I promise."

"Not unless they're deep fried and wrapped in bacon."

"All right, I'll bring your unhealthy pizza up in a bit."

"Hey, I earned at least two thousand calories of junk food this weekend."

"Good to have you back, Tess."

"It's good to be back." She flopped onto her white leather sofa. Now that she was back in her favorite place, the tension she'd felt since leaving Ben's office should relax, but if anything, she was even more tense.

She gazed around the apartment that had been her home since she was sixteen. She loved it. It was the first thing she'd ever had that was all hers. Bookshelves lined the walls on both sides of her living room. On one side, the shelves housed her television, opposite the large sofa, and on the other side, her bed. The kitchen and bathroom flanked the foyer entry, making it all one big space.

For one brief second, she let herself imagine having Dean here with her. Then she shut that line of thought down tight. She could not pine over a guy when she had so much work to do.

Waiting for her food to arrive, Tess fired up her iPad and did her weekly shopping. All the clothes, books, music, and gadgets she could find on Primely.com were hers for the taking. Everything she needed went on the Soma account and arrived at her door the next day. She practically had an unlimited budget, and rarely had an order Soma wouldn't approve. It was just too bad she couldn't charge her tuition and training fees to the account too. She lost herself in some guilt-free shopping, driving all thoughts of Dean from her mind.

Her phone beeped again.

"Ms. St. James?"

"Becky, hi," Tessa replied.

"Your new uniforms are ready. Should I have the concierge bring them up, or would you like to stop by for a fitting?"

"I'll stop by your shop tomorrow. Everything is always too long for me." The Soma uniforms were typical training gear: black fatigues tailored to a perfect fit with the Soma logo along the sleeve, just above her status rank within the hierarchy of the agency. Her newest uniforms marked her as a four star student with a third level training status, meaning she worked with the kids from the Fold on a weekly basis as a trainer. Only the most talented students could become trainers before becoming an agent.

“Perfect. I'll schedule you for a fitting on Wednesday. Shall I charge it to your account?”

"Yes, thank you, Becky." Tessa smiled as she ended the call. It really was a relief to be home. Every time she left for Amrita, it felt like traveling to another planet. The mortal world was so vastly different from her world. Venturing into it was always such a culture shock and coming home to Sterling Tower reminded her that Soma was her family. Always had been and always would be. She owed it to them all to make something of herself.

"Pizza's here!" Eric called from the foyer.

"Come in. I'm starving." Tessa scrambled off the sofa to meet him in the kitchen.

"You sit and eat; I'll put the groceries away," Eric ordered. "How was Cleveland?"

"Cold."

"And the fights?"

"Same game, different town." She shrugged.

"Give me something, Tess. Meet any hot guys?"

Her answering smile was the only reply Eric needed.

"Dish it."

"It's all anonymous, Eric. You know that," she insisted. "It was nothing."

"Nothing?"

"Absolutely nothing." The lie tasted bitter on her lips. Eric was the closest thing she had to a real friend, but she'd never let him get close enough to truly know her. There was no way she was telling him about Dean.

"Girl, we gotta get you a boyfriend."

"I don't have time for that."

"Tell me about it." He sighed as he put her groceries away. He was familiar with her home and how she liked her things arranged.

"How's school?" Eric was one of the few who actually got to go to college on campus and major in something useful.

He was going to be a Soma psychologist someday. Tessa was just a part-time, online student majoring in Liberal Arts. A basic degree that would give her the education she would need to perform her assignments. Her real education came in the training room and she usually preferred it that way. But sometimes she longed for the real college experience.

"Good. Classes are boring as hell, but the socializing is what I'm there for anyway." He winked.

"You have a perfect GPA. You know you like school."

"I do. But it would be nice if I could choose my own classes. I like psychology, but I'd rather focus on abnormal psych and go the route of the forensic psychologist. But the Soma gods want me preparing for child psych. So I do what I'm told."

Eric was never quite satisfied with life at Soma, but he was twenty-one years old and still lived in the dormitories. His job as a concierge barely paid for his training and he was tapped out on Soma loans for everything else. He didn't have it nearly as good as Tessa did.

"Well, I can't complain," she said. "They usually let me take the classes I want, except the language courses. I wanted to focus on learning as many languages as possible, but my Soma advisor said it's not important." Tessa shrugged. "Apparently, being multi-lingual isn't a necessity for what they have planned for me."

"Do you ever wonder what that is?" Eric asked, helping himself to a slice of her pizza.

"I'm anxious to find out, but I trust that whatever my

assignment will be, it will be suited to my gifts and the training I've had."

"Well, you are clearly destined for bigger and better things." He gestured at her home. "Maybe college isn't as big a deal for you right now."

"Exactly. There's always later. We won't be Soma students forever. Eventually we will be agents and have more time to do the things we want." She held onto that thought like a lifeline. Just because she couldn't be with Dean now, didn't mean they would never see each other again.

"From your lips to God's ears. I gotta get back to work. See you later." Eric left her to her quiet night alone with her pizza ... and thoughts of honey-brown eyes.

CHAPTER 4

The alarm blared loudly in the darkness, shrieking the most annoying music on Tessa's playlists. She wasn't a morning person. Especially a "it's still dark outside" kind of morning person.

"Shut up" she grunted at the voice activated alarm. "I'm up. I'm up." She brushed the sleep out of her eyes. Three-thirty was an ungodly hour, but she was determined to get to the warehouse before Chase to get in some early practice. She wanted to be warmed up by the time he arrived, so they could make the most of the time she was paying him.

She slipped into her black and red uniform with the Soma emblem on the shoulder. Just like the brand on her ankle. The one she received when she was sixteen. Under the red serpent clutching its own tail were three stars underlined with four red bars, marking rank. The new uniforms added a fourth star-the highest you could go as a student, moving her that much closer to the coveted fifth star. The agent star, which would earn her an assignment. She was so close she could taste it.

Tess was the only one out so early-really the middle of the night. Few were as dedicated as she was. She hit the elevator button for the basement level, swiping her ID card for access. The car dropped to the lowest level quickly with no stops along the way.

The warehouse was Tessa's favorite place to train. She loved sparring and honing her lesser gifts in the gym, but working with her signature gift-what she deemed her signature gift-was the most rewarding thing she did all week. Most saw her ability to thrive off of the strength of others during a fight as her most defining gift but Tessa disagreed. That was a party trick. Her elemental gift would be her career maker, and that was where her focus went. She preferred being in nature to practice. And that was what the warehouse offered.

"At it awfully early, Ms. St. James," the security guard said as she made her way through the tunnel connecting Sterling tower with the warehouse. She nodded. "I've got some time to make up after my trip." Amrita was her only source of income, but it took her away from her priorities every month. The time away was always an enormous set back.

"It's shaping up to be a beautiful day in there." He held the double doors open for her.

Tessa stepped onto the moss covered ground. The darkness of night just beginning to fade with the first rays of light spilling over the horizon. The sounds of the city never touched this place. That was her favorite part about her time here. It was like stepping into another dimension. From the exterior, the warehouse looked like any other boring building, but it belied the immensity of what it concealed.

Inside, was a world of forests, hills, lakes, and trees. Even a mountain with foothills and streams. Birds and all kinds of creatures lurked within its depths. Some gentle. Some not. The creation of such a fathomless world within the confines of the warehouse was thanks to the ancient Immortal who lived there. Harold didn't like to be bothered, but Tessa appreciated all he did to facilitate her training. He'd created a training center just for her. A small cabin surrounded with various levels of polluted ponds. Her job was to purify the water using her gift. She had been able to clear the murky ponds for some time now, but traces of toxins were still evident in her latest samples. She needed to be able to make the water safe to drink. A feat she was determined to conquer any day now.

As she made her way to the ponds at the base of the mountain, Tessa's thoughts were filled with grand ideas of a future visiting remote corners of the third world, cleaning the polluted and muddy waters, making them safe to drink for those without clean water.

She arrived an hour before she expected Chase, her palms itching to get to work. Chase's work station and chemistry paraphernalia were housed in the small cabin-a mini laboratory exclusively for the purposes of her training. She quickly had everything in place and her safety gloves and goggles on to collect her first samples. She could easily scoop up a bottle of water from the filthy pond and use her gift to make it safe to drink, but that was child's play. She'd been able to do that for two years. She needed to be able to restore an entire lake to pure, fresh water. Once she conquered the small ponds, she would be ready to tackle larger bodies of water.

Each of her ponds held a different range of pollutants. Every session, she would begin with the first pond and work her way through them all until she had samples from before and after the use of her gift. This morning she was using her "practice pond" until Chase arrived.

Tessa prepared her starter samples. Chase would compare them against her clean sample, giving them a baseline of what she needed to work on for the rest of their time together. Using her gift was both incredibly freeing and insanely difficult at the same time. Letting her power flood her body until she could practically see it crackling at her fingertips was one of the most euphoric sensations she'd ever experienced. In that moment, Tessa was at peace. But as she directed that power into the clouded, polluted waters of the pond, that sense of euphoria vanished. It was replaced with a feeling of loss and pain so profound it almost made her weep. She likened it to experiencing what nature felt in the presence of such pollution. As she fought to pull the toxins from the water and into herself, she could feel the toll it took on her body. Her gift allowed her to extract the various particulates in the water and absorb the contamination using her body's natural filtration system, leaving behind pure H2O, or that was the ultimate goal anyway. Years ago the ability left her feeling ill for days, but with time, she developed a tolerance to the toxins coursing through her body. Now, she only needed a few minutes to rest before she could use her gift again.

The pond water was clear now. Just like it had been for the last several months. But it probably still wasn't safe to drink. Once Chase tested it for toxins, she would know if she'd made any improvement since last time.

Tess stumbled to the cabin to rest on the front porch until Chase arrived. Hands trembling, she reached for a protein bar and a bottle of water from her pack. Using her gift still left her weak, but she recovered quickly.

Sweat dripped from her brow as she sat on the top step. The morning was warm and humid already, and the sun wasn't fully up yet. Harold's temperatures fluctuated drastically from day to day. This weather usually meant someone was being punished. There were always others here. She could sense them, even this early. Some chose to live here like Harold while they trained and honed their gifts in a natural setting. Others, like Tessa, came just for training, choosing to live in the comfort of Sterling Tower instead. And sometimes, the warehouse was used for punishment when rules were broken.

Tessa heard the furious pounding of footsteps along the pathway that lead to the top of the mountain. A treacherous climb from what she'd heard. She'd never been disciplined before, but she knew others who had received this particular punishment.

The footsteps neared, and she saw a familiar face. He resembled Dean so much more than she realized. The shock of it sent her heart lurching to her toes.

How can I miss him this much when I hardly know him?

Quinn was younger than his nephew by a few years, but much more serious than Dean. She would give anything to be in Livia's inner circle the way Quinn and Santi were. They got to live and train with her, yet they seemed to despise Livia for it. It was no secret how often they were penalized for their transgressions. This morning Quinn was running up the mountain as fast as his legs could carry him. He streaked past her, like he had a horde of demons chasing him. The look on his face was one of grim determination-and hate. He would not fail at whatever task he'd been set.

The incline was steep, and the way was rocky. Quinn slipped and couldn't regain his footing as he slid back down the path.

"Careful!" Tessa rushed to help him. She couldn't fathom the sheer look of terror in his eyes as he punched the ground, bloodying his knuckles in frustration. She faltered in her steps, wondering what he could possibly have done to deserve whatever had put that look on his face.

She wrapped her arm around his waist and lifted his

arm over her shoulder. He flinched at her touch, like he hadn't realized she was there.

"Take it easy, Quinn," she said softly. He leaned heavily on her as she helped him get back on his feet.

"Every second counts." His tortured voice was like a knife in her gut. "I won't let her go back to Michael. Not after last time."

"Shhhh." Tessa squeezed his hand and offered him her water bottle. "Go." She pointed him toward the path. "Perform the task you've been given and put it behind you at the end of the day. It's the only way to get through the difficult times."

"Thank you." He gave her a quizzical look, like he wasn't sure she was real. "I forgot what kindness looks like in this place."

As she watched him move up the path and disappear in the distance, she felt a stab of guilt. Part of her wanted to tell him his family was looking for him. That they didn't want him to be here. Yet she wouldn't tell him. He'd made his decision when he came to Soma for help.

Keep your nose out of it, St. James. It's none of your business. But something about Quinn's demeanor didn't sit well with her. If he didn't want to be here, why didn't he just leave?

"These samples aren't any better than the ones you've been producing for the last few months, Tess." Chase poured the crystal clear water onto the ground. "We're not making the kind of progress we need to be making if you want to get your assignment anytime soon. I'm thinking of recommending another year of training."

"Please. No." Tess closed her eyes with a shiver. "Anything but that."

"Most students your age aren't ready to leave training yet. If you need another year, take it. But if you want to get ahead, then you need to be working harder and practicing more. Maybe we should meet daily if you want to pick up the pace."

At the rate she was spending money, she'd have to add another year at Amrita even after she'd taken her first assignment. That thought nearly killed her. She only had three months left, and she was finally out of there.

"Can we identify what toxins are still present? And then maybe I can focus on understanding those, so I can have a better idea of how to extract them with my gift?"

"I'll have to put some research time into it."

"How much will that cost?" She winced.

"My regular hourly rate for maybe ten or twelve hours of research."

Tessa nodded. It would take half of her winnings from the next Amrita to make that happen, but she had to do it. Maybe her mother would understand if she didn't send money this month. She'd have to tell her Soma financial advisor to stop the automatic deposit into her mother's account. Just this once. She'd make it up later.

"Fine. Let's do it."

"Wire the money, and I'll get on it tonight. We will figure this out, Tess. I promise. I have faith in you and your ability to produce results."

"I know. I just need to work harder before our meeting with Livia next month."

"You have to be ready to knock her socks off."

"Oh, I'll be ready if it kills me."

"You're co-training with Santi today." Eric passed the clipboard to Tessa to log her time for the Fold payroll. Not that it paid much. She always used her monthly paycheck to tip the Soma staff for all their hard work. Whatever was left, she put in her paltry savings account.

"I'm pretty sure Santi hates me." Tessa scribbled her name on the sign-in sheet.

"I'm pretty sure Santi hates everyone," Eric said.

"If I had Livia's ear the way she does, I'd be the happiest person in Soma."

"You *are* the happiest person in Soma." Eric gave her a wink.

"What can I say, Friday is my favorite work day." She smiled. "I get to train the two cutest kids in the world."

"Watch out for Lennox. She kicks."

"And bites." Tessa laughed. Lennox was her favorite student, but the girl had anger issues. She'd grown up in Soma the way Tess had, but she struggled to get along with the other kids. That was why Tessa worked with her regularly. Lennox's teachers in the Fold wanted Tessa to help her see how much of an advantage living and training at Soma could be. But the girl was lonely. Her only friend was Hunter, and she tolerated him at best.

"Have a good day!" Eric called as the elevator arrived to take her to the tenth floor.

Lennox was a bully. And Tessa wasn't sure Santi was the best influence. She stepped into the cool lobby of the Fold, swiping her access card to enter the classroom wing. Her training with Lennox and Hunter wasn't physical. It was something of a social sciences class.

"Good morning," Tessa greeted the sullen Santi. The other woman had dark circles under her eyes, and she crossed the room with a limp.

"Let's just get this done." Santi dragged four small desks into a circle. "I have a mountain to climb later today." Like Quinn, Santi was always in trouble.

"You know if you follow the rules here, it's really a great place to train."

"You're an absolute moron if you believe that." Santi slid into her desk with a wince.

"Whatever. The kids will be here in a minute. Let's just try to make this fun for them?"

"I'd rather run up a mountain than work here. This place is ... a whole different kind of torture."

"You don't like kids?"

"That's not it." Santi gave her a haunted look.

"Tessa!" Hunter rushed into the room to give her a big hug. The twelve year old boy was a gentle soul. He probably wouldn't prove to be as talented as Lennox, but the two kids worked well together, so their teachers liked to keep them in the same classes. Mainly because Hunter tempered Lennox's behavior. Some of the other boys picked on Hunter, and Len took her bodyguard duties seriously. If anyone messed with Hunter, they'd have to deal with her.

"Where's Len?"

"Right here." Lennox trudged into the room. She hated any class that required her to sit at a desk. She'd rather spend her time sparring and working out in the gym than cracking open a book.

"No books in this class today, Lennox. You can wipe that frown off your face." Santi smiled at the girl. The smile transformed her face entirely. She loved Lennox as much as Tessa did.

"What are you doing here?" Lennox asked, climbing into her seat beside Santi. "Are you teaching here now?"

"Sometimes when my schedule allows it."

"What are you teaching us today?" Hunter asked.

"Not sure. I think Ms. St. James has a plan. Though I'm not sure how I'm supposed to contribute."

"This is more like your counseling sessions with James.

We're just going to talk today, and Santi will weigh in with her perspective."

"Boring." Lennox sighed.

"You think going to a real school would be any more exciting?" Santi asked.

"Yes. At least at a real school there are more kids and less fighting."

"This is a real school," Tessa said. "And fighting is like recess to you."

"At a *real* school, we'd get to go outside between lessons and then go home to families at the end of the day," Lennox said sadly.

"I remember going to a regular school when I was a little kid," Tessa said. "I learned the important things. Math, reading, science, and history. But I didn't learn anything about being Immortal. That's why I came here when I was eight, and I've been here ever since. I can't imagine training anywhere else."

"But most kids train with their parents at home," Hunter said.

"That's kind of the old fashioned way of doing it. Many families stubbornly stick to old training methods that don't really work anymore. It was fine for our parents and grandparents, but those of us born in this modern world have gifts they don't understand. We desperately needed a place like Soma to teach us. That is why we are all here."

Santi made a low disgusted noise and crossed her legs under the table. She sat there with her arms folded across her chest and her mouth a fine line of tension, like she was having trouble holding her tongue.

"You disagree, Ms. Santiago?"

"Yes. I trained at home my whole life with my ancient parents and grandparents. I also have a more modern gift they didn't quite understand. But they never stopped trying to help me. And they never stubbornly stuck to the old ways."

"And yet, you have come here to train?" Once again, Tessa couldn't understand why someone like Santi, who obviously didn't want to be here, didn't just leave if Soma turned out to be more than she could handle.

Santi's face clouded with confusion. "I suppose there are ... circumstances about my place here that I can't really discuss freely."

"The point is, kids, you are in the best place you could possibly be at your age. You will be so much better prepared for your Awakening when that time comes. You'll hit the ground running and make so much more progress than you ever would at home. For some kids who opt to train at home, or are not talented enough to get into Soma, it takes years to make the kind of progress we make in weeks or months here."

"That's not entirely true, Tessa," Santi said.

"You don't think we can ensure a newly Awakened Immortal can learn to control their gift in a matter of weeks? I've seen it done. Many times."

"So have I. At home. You make it sound like training at home would take years to learn to control a gift."

"In the majority of cases it does, Santi. Your experiences might be different because you are a very powerful woman, but those without your talent can struggle for years to attain the kind of control we teach our youngest students in weeks."

"I would question where you're getting your information," Santi mumbled.

"Statistics don't lie."

"Made up ones do."

"We are getting off track." Tessa sighed. "The point of our lesson today is to remind you that while life at Soma can be difficult, and our expectations are high, you will receive the absolute best education in the world. And one day, when you've achieved the goals set for you by you instructors, you will walk out of here with so many opportunities you never would have training at home."

Santi shot her a glare so cold, it sent a shiver through Tessa's body. She might not believe what Tessa was teaching these kids, but at least she was holding her tongue for the moment.

"You'll have plenty of time for fun and goofing off a bit later in life. Right now it's important to start thinking about your future. My mother works her fingers to the bone to get by. She's never had the advantages I've had. She never stops working. Imagine holding down two full-time jobs? She teaches school in the mornings and works at a factory on second shift and weekends. And she's done that for more than a hundred years. Rarely takes time off. Never takes a vacation. Her life will always be like that. At least until I make agent, and I'm able to take care of her for a change. That day is coming soon, and we'll both know the separation has been worth it."

Santi's face softened. "I can relate. My family has struggled much the same as Tessa's. I just don't think Soma is the only answer to that problem. Taking a child away from their family deprives them of too much."

"I beg to differ," Tessa said. "You have a successful example sitting right in front of you. I miss my mother every day, but she and I are in this together."

"When's the last time you actually talked to your mom? The way I see it, you don't know what you've missed by not being with her during the last very important decade of your life."

"It's not like I even have a mom," Lennox said. "But I guess walking out of here with a decent future ahead of me sounds good."

"It'll work out for you, kid," Santi said. "And when you have your own kids some day, you'll be able to teach them all the fancy stuff you've learned here."

"We're going to have two kids. A boy and a girl," Hunter said. "And we'll live at the top floor of Sterling Tower."

"You are deluded if you think I'm going to marry anyone," Lennox said. "And I'm going to live at the beach. I've never seen the ocean, but it looks awesome on TV. A place with sand, sun, and all the fresh air you can handle has to be a fun place to live."

"One of these days, Quinn and I will take you there." Santi tucked a stand of stray hair behind her ear.

"Can I live with you guys?"

"And me too?" Hunter said.

"Let's take it one day at a time, kids," Tessa said. She didn't want Santi promising them anything she'd never be able to deliver.

"So from now on, we're going to study hard, practice daily, and always remember you're both just a few short years away from your Awakening. The most important thing you can do for yourself, especially you, Lennox, is to graduate from the Fold with an invitation into Soma's higher education program."

"Otherwise, we get sent home, right?" Hunter asked.

"Unfortunately, not everyone can earn a place at Soma."

"What will happen to me if I don't make it to Soma?" Lennox asked.

"Let's just cross that bridge when we get there." Tessa couldn't look the girl in the eye. She would likely never make it into Soma, though Tess hoped she could pull it off. Tessa was one of only a few who knew Lennox had recently experienced an early Awakening. If her teachers ever discovered it, she would be expelled from the Fold and have no hope of entering Soma. This world was no place for a girl with no future. But Tessa hoped and prayed Lennox could make it here a few more years. She had no where else to go.

"Hey." Santi leaned forward and grabbed Len's hands, giving them a gentle squeeze. "I don't want you worrying about that, okay? We will take care of you," she whispered. "All of us."

"Okay, kids!" Tessa clapped her hands. "Ms. Mason is waiting for you in the warehouse. Have fun out there."

Lennox and Hunter raced out of the room. Playing in the warehouse was their reward for a good week in class.

"Are you really so blind you can't see how much those two are missing?" Santi folded her arms across her chest.

"Sacrifices now will give them a head start later." Tessa gathered her things. She had an appointment with her physical trainer in the gym and talking to Santi made her nervous. "We live a hard life here, but Hunter's parents want a better life for him and Lennox needs Soma if she's going to have any kind of future at all. You may not agree, but I've seen the good this place can do. In the future, I would appreciate it if you wouldn't undermine my authority in my classroom."

"You know it just as well as I do, don't you? You work with Lennox all the time. She loves you."

"Know what?"

"That girl's days here are numbered. It's only a matter of time before they kick her out."

"Lennox will rally. She's a tough girl."

"She's a thirteen-year-old child with no family and the limitations of an early Awakening. Where do you think she's going to go?"

"Let's just hope she can fly under the radar for a few more years. She doesn't have much of a chance at succeeding here, but it's the only chance she's got."

"Are you even listening to yourself? I thought I was naive when I came here, but you're really a product of your environment."

"I feel bad for Lennox. I really do. But filling her head with promises we can't keep isn't going to help her. The best chance she has is to make it here a little longer until she's old enough to take care of herself." And when the time comes, I'm going to help her. Tess refused to leave the kid with nothing. She fully intended to send Lennox to her mother in the event she was expelled. But Tessa couldn't help but think Santi had a point. Her perspective on Soma had Tessa questioning things she'd always accepted as fact. Santi grew up with a powerful family around her. They trained her well, despite their limitations and traditional ways. But they clearly loved her. Whatever Santi came looking for from Soma, she hadn't found it. Tessa just wondered what was keeping her here.

"I feel sorry for you." Santi shook her head. "But I have a mountain to climb."

"Do you trust me?" James asked.

Tessa nearly jumped out of her skin when she closed her apartment door behind her. "You scared the shit out of me! What are you doing here? How are you even get in? I locked it."

"I got Eric to let me in. He has a major crush on me."

"So why not go out with him instead of breaking into my house?"

"I have other things I'm dealing with at the moment."

"I haven't seen you much the last few weeks." She took a seat beside him on the sofa. He didn't look so good. "Is everything okay?"

"Stressful times. The last Amrita didn't go too well for me. Recruits were low, so I'm off the circuit 'til next year."

"I wish I could get off the circuit," she muttered.

"And what would you do for money?"

"Good point. I wish I could offer you a loan, but money is tight for me right now with all my extra training."

"I'll be okay. That's not why I'm here. Do you trust me?"

"You know I do."

"Enough to help me break all the rules ... ever?"

Tessa gave him a hard stare. He was a total wreck. Hands shaking, with sweat beading at his temple. "What's going on, James? You know you can count on me."

"It's Lennox."

"What about her? I just had her in my class two weeks ago and she seemed fine." But she wouldn't doubt if some of what Santi had said upset her.

"We have to get her out of here. It's not safe for her anymore."

"They found out?" All the color rushed from Tessa's face. She'd really thought they could get her through the next couple of years before they would have to face this.

"We've been hiding it as best we can, but Livia and Ryan know about her early Awakening. They're going to put her into the mortal foster system."

"That's ... inhumane. What about her parents? I always thought they would come back for her under the circumstances." "

They signed over their parental rights to Soma years ago. Foster care is protocol in this situation."

"She'll just run away the first chance she gets; everyone

knows that. You're right. We have to get her out of here," Tessa said.

"Will you help me?" James asked.

"Of course."

"You've always been such a stickler for the rules."

"I know, but I've been keeping Len's secret. I love that kid and I can't let her go into foster care. That's not the answer. I can't imagine what Livia is thinking."

"Livia doesn't always have a choice either," James said softly.

"I can send Lennox to my mother," Tess offered. "That's sort of what I've planned for her anyway."

"Trust me when I say we need to make Lennox disappear."

Tess nodded. She felt the urge not to ask too many questions and of all the people at Soma, she trusted James the most. "All right, what do you need me to do?"

"I'm leaving with Lennox on Thursday, during all the hustle and bustle of Amrita prep. Everyone expects me to be leaving with the team, but I'm suspended. I should be able to get past security with my suitcase, but I need you to sneak her out of the building in yours. They always stop me at security, and I can't take the chance that they might do a bag search. But you're the Soma golden child. You skate through security all the time. I'm counting on the fact that they never check your suitcase."

"What if they do this time?"

"Have they ever?"

"No," she admitted.

"You love it here, Tess. You're their poster child for the way this place is supposed to work. I can't believe you don't realize it, but you get whatever you want, whenever you want it."

"You make it sound like I have it easy." Tessa bristled at the insinuation that she somehow didn't have to work as hard as everyone else.

"No one questions how hard you work. You deserve your rank and everything that comes with it. That's what Lennox needs from you—your unquestionable status."

"So I get her out of the building and meet you?" Tessa heaved a big sigh. She didn't like this, but she liked the thought of Lennox in foster care even less.

"I'll be waiting for you at the coffee cart near the park. I'll have your real suitcase. If they happen to search my bag and find girly things, I can blow it off like I grabbed the wrong bag since we all have the same luggage. That's a corner I can talk myself out of. A child in my suitcase, I can't. Once we meet, we'll make the switch, and no one will notice she's gone until it's too late. Then you go on to Amrita like always."

"Where will you take her?"

"I have some friends helping. We're going to find her a real home," James replied.

"When will you be back? They'll wonder where you've gone," she said.

"I'm not coming back, Tessa. I can't explain, but Soma has become a dangerous place for me. I need to go."

"Dangerous?" Tessa frowned. "Life here is hard, but I wouldn't call it dangerous." She understood the compulsion to leave. Not everyone made it through to agent status. But dangerous?

"Not all of us can be the kind of rising star you are, little Tessie." James smiled at her fondly.

Tess nodded uncertainly. "Be careful, James. I'll miss you." She leaned over to hug him. "I'm not sure I can imagine Soma without you."

"Not everything is as it seems." He hugged her tight. "Don't let your ambition cloud your judgment.

More and more, Tessa was seeing things at Soma as she never had before. Questioning her world, trying to make sense out of things that made no sense.

"You will trust in yourself, Tessa St. James." His voice took on a formal note. Far too serious for James. "The child of prophecy needs you. Trials lie ahead for us all but especially for you. Circumstances will tear you down to the studs, only to build you back up again. Open your eyes, Tess."

"What was that?" She stared at him, his eyes glowing with the dim light of his power.

"Just call it a tiny bit of advice from someone who loves you."

"It's this or foster care. Get in the damn bag, Lennox," James insisted.

"I'm way too big to fit in there. How will I breathe?" Lennox's voice squeaked in fear.

"It's a cloth bag, sweetheart. You'll be fine. I promise," Tessa said.

Lennox shook her head. "I don't want to get in the bag." She took a step back.

"You know why we have to do this, Len. Now get in the damn bag," James said.

"James, give her a break." Tess glared at him. "It'll be just a quick ride to the park, and then you can get out."

"And then I'll have a new home?" Lennox stared up at James. "With parents? And school like you promised?"

"Yes."

Tess hoped it wasn't a lie. She hoped Lennox would get the most perfect childhood there ever was, wherever she was going.

"Who knows, maybe one day we'll see each other again." Tessa smiled.

"Okay, I'm gettin' in the damn bag." Lennox crouched in the suitcase on the floor and curled into a ball. "You just better be fast, Tess. I don't like this."

"Remember to be quiet and still," James said.

"I'll meet you there in a few minutes," Tess said, wheeling the suitcase with Lennox into the hallway.

"Take care of yourself, Tessa," James said. "This place ... It's not everything our world has to offer."

"It's a hard life, and it's not for everyone. I'll make the most of it. I always do."

"Let's get this show on the road already. I'm dying in here." Len's voice was muffled but clearly irritated at their lingering sentiments.

Tessa nervously walked to the elevator as James took the stairs back down to his office where he had her real suitcase stored.

"Have a good trip, Tess!" Eric called from his station at the front desk lobby. "They're gathering outside to load the van to the airport. You're early. You want a cup of coffee?"

"No, thanks. I'll take a walk over to the park."

"Leave your suitcase here. I'll make sure it gets loaded."
"I'm good, thanks," Tess said in a rush as she swept through the doors at the security checkpoint. James was right: they never checked her credentials at the door. Most of the guards were used to seeing her come and go as she pleased.

"Have a good trip, Ms. St. James," the head of security said, tipping his hat to her.

"Thanks, Robert." She flashed a smile as she stepped through the doors and into the fresh, crisp Atlanta fall.

Once she was across the street, she picked up her pace.

"It's cold," Lennox whispered.

"Almost there, kiddo. You're doing a great job."

"Tessa?" Lennox said.

"What is it, sweetheart?"

"Keep an eye on Hunter for me? The kids pick on him."

"I will. You just worry about yourself."

Tessa stepped around the corner to find James waiting impatiently for her in front of the coffee cart.

"Thanks for doing this," he whispered. "You have no idea how grateful I am." He handed her a cup of coffee like they were just friends meeting for a quick cup and a chat. They walked to a car parked on the street and seamlessly switched suitcases. He lifted Lennox into the back seat, easing open the zipper enough so she could get herself out of it when it was safe. James turned and gave Tess a hug.

"You take care of our girl, James. She's special."

"I will. You take care of yourself."

With that Tessa turned and taking a sip of her coffee, she walked back to Sterling Tower feeling a little lost. It was the second time in as many months that she had defied Soma. It was becoming a bad habit. But she could no longer deny that there were things about Soma that just didn't add up anymore. This business with Lennox crossed a line with her. The kid deserved more from the people who'd raised her. She just hoped James was able to follow through on his promises.

"There she is," the Soma driver called. "Ms. St. James, just the one we were waiting for." His smile was wide and genuine.

"Mr. Owen, it's good to see you. Sorry to keep you waiting." She lifted her coffee cup.

"And you didn't bring me one?"

"Next time." She grinned and slid into the front seat. It was time to do her job now. After this trip, she only had one more. The end of her stint in the arenas was coming to a close.

"Where you going this time?" Mr. Owen whispered. She wasn't supposed to disclose any details about Amrita, but he enjoyed hearing about the places she got to visit.

"Spain." She was looking forward to a few nights in Barcelona. Maybe she'd get her head on straight while she was gone. Ever since that night with Dean, she'd lost her focus, and it was time to get it back. She had one more star to earn.

Three days. Amrita only kept her away from Soma for three days, but it felt like a lifetime. The fights exhausted her physically, and the parties exhausted her mentally, but she desperately needed that fat paycheck for all the extra training time she'd booked with Chase.

Tessa walked through the front doors of Sterling Tower feeling like a new woman. Barcelona was amazing. Amrita was the same old game, and she was eager to get back to what mattered. She only had a few days to prepare for her quarterly meeting with Livia, and she intended to impress her with all the progress she'd made since their last meeting.

"Heya, Eric!" Tessa beamed at her friend as she stepped into the lobby, feeling like this homecoming was more exciting than usual.

"You're expected in Livia's office right now." He looked worried, and like he hadn't slept at all since she left.

"Now?" Her breath caught. She so wasn't ready. She needed at least one more session with Chase before she would feel even remotely prepared to face her boss.

"There's been a ... changing of the guard while you were gone," he whispered, glancing at the lobby cameras. "Livia's missing."

"What? Missing, how?"

"I don't know. She left the same day you left for Amrita. She took Quinn and Santi with her. None of them have returned. James and Lennox are missing, too."

"It's only been three days. I'm sure it's—"

Eric shook his head. "We have a new director. He's waiting for you now."

"Who is it?"

"I think this ... I think this might be a good thing, Tess."

Tessa raced up to her apartment to drop off her bags and rushed to Livia's pristine office. Except it wasn't so pristine. Boxes and duffle bags lay scattered about the room, like someone lost interest taking over Livia's space. He sat at the desk with his back to her, his worn boots propped up on the white marble console table.

It can't be! He'd never want this job.

"Tess! You're back." His broad smile lit his face, marred only slightly by the aged Soma tattoo on his cheek.

"Jayesh?" She rushed across the room to hug him. He'd

been like a big brother to her for most of her life, but she rarely got to see him since he left his position at Soma to head up a special forces team of seasoned agents. She'd like nothing more than to work directly for him one day. "You're taking over until Livia gets back?"

"That might not be any time soon. I'm your new boss, for now."

"What happened to Livia?"

"Not sure." He shrugged. "The big boss called me and here I am."

"You wanted to see me?" She sat on the chair in front of his desk, twisting her hands in her lap.

"Yes. I have an assignment for you. They've been waiting patiently for your training to be complete."

"I'm not ready." She shook her head. "Maybe in a few more months."

"You're ready." He frowned. "You've been ready for a while now. I have some good news and some bad news." He slid a folder across the desk. "The good news is your gift works perfectly. You've been removing all traces of toxins from larger bodies of water for nearly a year. Your specimens have been perfectly safe to drink. The bad news is your trainer, Chase, has been fleecing you for a lot of unnecessary training hours. You've paid him thousands for training and research you didn't need."

Tess shook her head again. "No. Chase would never do that to me."

"The proof is right there in front of you, sweetheart. As well as a sizable check to reimburse you for every penny he stole from you."

Tessa's hands shook as she opened the folder. The lab results of the last year of her work didn't lie. Chase-someone she trusted with the most important aspects of her training-had lied to her. He saw her as a cash cow and took advantage of her trust. The cashier's check came straight from Chase's bank account. Every dime she'd given him for a year, he'd returned in full. The enormity of the amount of money she held in her hand stunned her. How had she paid him so much?

"He agreed to return the money?" She cast her eyes up at Jayesh. He sat on the desk in front of her, a sad frown on his face.

"Selena can be very convincing."

"You had her threaten to take his gift?"

"He was all too eager to empty his bank accounts to avoid a date with her."

"Thank you. Jayesh ... I don't even know what to say. I'm so stupid." She was crushed. She should have seen it. The way Chase charged her for every little thing.

"No, you trusted your trainer as you should. It is Soma's fault for allowing such a thing to happen to you. We will be keeping a better eye on you now."

"So, you're giving me my first assignment?"

"I am."

"Am I really ready?" She couldn't believe this was happening so quickly. Her pulse pounded in her ears, terrified and elated at the same time.

"You have to be. This isn't going to be an easy first task for you. But I know you can do it."

"I absolutely can." She sat up straighter. "When do I leave? Where am I going?" Excitement flushed her face as her mind whirled with all the things she needed to do before she left.

"You will leave for South America next week. Until then, you need to spend every free moment preparing your new student for this assignment."

"My student?" She'd never heard of a student going on an assignment. If that were a possibility, she would have been given that opportunity long ago.

"Yes. A special case. We've recently discovered a new recruit with an environmental gift like yours. I believe you two will work so well together for this assignment that I had to make an exception. It will be your job to continue your student's training in addition to your new responsibilities. I've ensured your new employer you are up to the challenge."

"I've trained all my life for this. How can a new recruit possibly be ready? It isn't fair."

"Fair? Nothing about what we do is fair, Tessa," Jayesh said softly. "You and your student are needed for a very important job. It is as simple as that."

"You're right. I will not fail either task. When will I get to meet this recruit?"

"Right now." Jayesh leaned over his desk to reach for the phone. "Ryan, send him in, please."

"Unfortunately, your student has had a little trouble adjusting to Soma's higher expectations. You will counsel him through this difficult time. Teach him that Soma is here to help him become the best he can be."

Tessa hesitated to turn when the door opened behind her, and her student stepped into the room. All her life, she'd dreamed of the moment when she would finally become a real agent. And now she had to share that with someone else. It wasn't at all like she'd planned, but she would roll with it.

"Tessa?" His voice no longer carried that teasing tone that haunted her dreams, but the sound of her name on his lips sent her heart racing.

"Dean?" She turned to find her student could barely hold himself upright. Ryan shouldered him across the room, easing him into the chair beside her. Dean's face was bruised, and his right eye was nearly swollen shut. She almost didn't recognize him.

"What's happened to you?" She lunged from her seat to kneel beside him. "What are you doing here?" Her hands fluttered uselessly in her lap. She wanted to touch him, but she didn't want to hurt him.

"I take it you two have met before?" Jayesh said.

She nodded. "Amrita. Two months ago. Why does he

look like he's gone through a meat-grinder, Jayesh? What is the meaning of this?"

"He's had a rough few days, but he knows what is expected of him now."

"This is not one of your military operations. We don't treat people like this! I'm so sorry, Dean. This isn't right."

"This?" Dean scowled at her. "Isn't this what you wanted, Tessa? Or is that even your real name?"

"Of course it is," she whispered, reaching for his hand. But Dean pulled away.

"I trust if you're old friends, then there should be very little trouble getting Dean settled?" Jayesh continued, not giving her an actual answer about Dean's condition.

"He will stay in the solitary dormitories until you leave for your assignment."

"He will stay with me until his face doesn't look like that anymore. And then if he wants to leave, he leaves." She stood to face Jayesh. He needed to understand that this was unacceptable. This was not the way they handled the students who came to them for help.

"Dean is here of his own volition, aren't you, Dean?" Jayesh leaned over Livia's desk to give her a level look.

"Yeah. I signed up for the fast track," Dean muttered. "I just didn't realize you'd be teaching me."

"If he doesn't want to train with me, he shouldn't have to." Tessa couldn't look Dean in the eye. She'd longed to see him again. But not like this. He blames me. Tessa couldn't fathom why he would think any of this was her fault.

"You two need to work out your differences, and get yourselves focused on the job you both signed up for."

"Who is our new employer?" Tessa finally asked.

"Vivian Dyson and her Complement, Fletcher.

"Michael and Ryan's mother? That Vivian Dyson?" She and her Complement ran Valkyrie Enterprises, a Fortune 500 company. They also ran a non-profit organization dedicated to improving the environment. Tessa couldn't have hand selected a better first assignment. The rainforests of South America were exactly where she and her gift belonged.

"Ryan will escort you to her complex in a remote part of the Columbian jungle in just a few days. That gives you two some time to get reacquainted. You are dismissed. Dean, you will go with Ms. St. James. She will get you settled. Remember everything we've discussed?" Jayesh gave him a lingering gaze.

Dean nodded. "I've got it under control, Jayesh. Thank you for all you've done for me and my family."

Jayesh nodded. "I wish I could have done more."

Tessa didn't like the vacant, lifeless look in Dean's eyes, nor the odd exchange between the two men.

Tessa helped Dean to his feet and led him silently from Jayesh's office. She had no idea where to go from here, but she wouldn't lose focus on what was important. She'd finally received her first assignment. She would have to deal with the fact that Dean seemed to despise her now. Whatever had passed between them before needed to stay in the past.

"You can sleep in my bed until you're feeling better. I'll sleep on the couch." Tessa helped Dean into her apartment. The silence between them was deafening.

Maybe I should have taken him to the solitary dorms. But she couldn't do that to him. Those rooms were like prison cells.

"I'll take the couch." Dean gingerly lowered himself onto the white leather. "Nice place."

His demeanor changed the moment they stepped into her home. She couldn't tell if he was actually glad to be here or if he still hated her. She busied herself with calling the front desk to avoid making eye contact.

"Eric, hi. Can you please send up a new recruit bag with clothes and toiletries for a man?"

"Seriously?" Eric's voice went up three octaves. She imagined his eyebrows shot right up to his hair line, too.

"Yes. Sizes should be large, and he's pretty tall, too."

"Seriously? Tessa, what the hell happened in that meeting?"

"Just send up the bag, please? And a first-aid kit."

"Oh, I'm coming right up."

Tessa ended the call and grabbed an icepack from the freezer.

"Put this on your eye. It'll help with the swelling." She couldn't understand why he wasn't healing on his own, and she didn't want to think about all the ways one might keep an Immortal from healing. Or why anyone at Soma would resort to such brutal means with a new recruit. What could Dean have possibly done to deserve this?

"Tessa." Dean grabbed her hand. "I know this isn't your fault."

She sat on the coffee table in front of him, relief flooding her body.

"You seemed so angry with me."

"I didn't want you to get in trouble for not recruiting me when you were supposed to."

"Why are you here?" She placed her hand over his. "Why does your face look like that?"

"I thought you liked my face?"

"This isn't a joke." Her eyes burned with the threat of tears.

"It's okay, Tessa. Let's just say this was the better choice of two evils, and I'm not super excited about being here. But I *am* happy to see you again."

"I don't understand this." She brushed his bruised face with her fingertips. "I've never seen anyone treated this way before."

"Don't concern yourself with it. There were ... extenuating circumstances you don't need to know about."

"You're really coming on assignment with me?" She would get to see him everyday. Her heart fluttered with the possibilities, and then her hopes sank like a stone in her stomach. This couldn't happen. Not now.

"Looks that way." He held her hands, massaging her palms with the pads of his thumb.

"Listen. I-I've worked for years to get where I am now." It took everything she had, but she pulled her hands away. "I can't have any distractions."

"I understand." Dean lay back against the sofa with a sigh.

"You should never have come to Amrita," she whispered. "I'm so sorry. You caught their attention. They can be relentless in their recruiting." Who was she fooling? She knew when Soma wanted someone, they got them. And Dean's face was all the proof she needed to see just how far they would go to collect a new recruit.

"This has nothing to do with Amrita, Tessa. Please don't worry about me. Let's start fresh. Get a few things straight." He sat up.

"I am your student. I'm sure there is a lot I can learn from you. When we are working, we will be professionally distant. Courteous and polite. Nothing more. But when we are alone, let there be no pretenses. We are friends. Allies." He took her hand again. "It doesn't have to be anything more than that."

She didn't know how he understood her position, but he got it, and she appreciated his honesty. "Where we are going, we will need to present a united front. Completely professional and we must stick to our roles. I am the teacher, and you are the student."

"Understood." He nodded. "And anything that

happened before tonight doesn't matter. Except that one night at Amrita. That still matters a great deal to me."

"Agreed." She stood at the soft knock on the door. She understood Dean was asking her not to ask any questions about his arrival. She could give him that. But there were too many things about Soma lately that just didn't add up. And this was one she wasn't sure she could overlook.

"Thanks, Eric." She grabbed the new recruit bag and tried to shut the door in his face.

"Come on, Tess," Eric protested. "You gotta give me something."

"I have a new student. He's injured. I'll talk to you tomorrow." She slammed the door shut, feeling only a little guilty for her rudeness. She just couldn't deal with Eric tonight.

"How about a hot shower and a change of clothes before bed?" Tessa asked.

"Depends." Dean cocked his head. "Will you be joining me?"

"I will not." She dropped the duffel bag into his lap with a smile. "There's a first-aid kit in there if you need it. Bathroom's through there." She pointed at the door. "Towels are in the cabinet. Help yourself."

"Worth a shot." He struggled to his feet. "I'll be good as new after some food and a good sleep."

"I'll make us some sandwiches." Tessa stepped into the kitchen and busied herself with making dinner. She needed to occupy her hands and her mind. There was so much to do to prepare for this assignment. She couldn't let herself get caught up in thoughts of Dean and a hot, steamy shower.

"That is one amazing shower." Dean joined her at the bar, smelling fresh and clean. "The extra jets really come in handy after a hard day training." She set a plate of warm panini style sandwiches between them. She'd managed a decent salad and fresh fruit plate, too. Dean needed clean, wholesome foods to help him heal. They had a huge day tomorrow, and she needed him back in shape.

"What's the plan? I can hear the wheels spinning in your head."

"We'll begin training at five a.m., so you need to get a good night's rest. I insist you take my bed, at least for tonight. I probably won't sleep much anyway."

"Well, if you insist." His wry smile gave her goose bumps. She had to get past these ridiculous reactions to having him near. She could not show up at her new job drooling over her student.

Three days? How can so much happen in three short days? While she was gone, her entire world changed. She was about to set off for South America with the guy she was madly crushing on to do a job she'd trained for her whole life.

"Jayesh said your gift was a lot like mine. How does it work?" In all of the chaos of his arrival, she'd failed to ask why she needed Dean to perform this job. Jayesh said it was an environmental gift-further evidence that they were indeed equals as Dean had claimed the night they met.

"We're equals, Tessa. It makes sense that our gifts would be similar. But you'll find out soon enough."

What happens when your equal becomes your student? A student you can't stop thinking about?

Chapter 7

Tessa gazed across the grassy hills, waiting for Dean to arrive. He was more than twenty minutes late. She couldn't let him get away with that. They could be friends, yes, but he had to understand she was in charge. Giving him too much leeway now would only set a bad precedent later. Once they arrived in South America, Tessa and Dean needed to have their individual roles down pat. It wouldn't do to have an unruly student who couldn't follow the most basic rules.

For the last three days, they'd focused on working in the gym to get Dean back up to his regular performance. He'd done extremely well, and she had such high hopes for their future together-as partners. It couldn't be more than that. Not while they were on assignment. As tempting as it was to think about the possibilities between them, she had to stay focused. After they returned ... who knew what that future held.

"I expect you to be on time to our lessons, Dean." She stood to greet him as he shuffled along the path to the cabin where Tess had trained for years.

"Sorry. I got cornered by Eric and all his questions. I just needed directions to find this place." He took a seat beside her on the top step. "I forgot which way to go once I hit the basement. And then I was pretty impressed once I got here. I've seen places like this before, but this is really something."

"Really? I've never heard of another place quite like the warehouse," Tessa said.

"My family has a terrarium. It's on a much smaller scale, though. Definitely doesn't have mountains."

"Do you really think your training has prepared you for what we are about to walk into?" she asked.

"I've had the best training you could possibly imagine." Tessa was certain Dean thought he was ready, but she couldn't wrap her mind around that possibility. It went against everything she was taught. There was just no way a new recruit could be prepared for an assignment so soon.

"You know I need you to be better than good?" It worried her that she really didn't know what he could do, how well he could do it, or what would be expected of him when they arrived at Valkyrie Enterprises. Tessa was the girl with the plan, and right now she had no plan at all.

"Trust me, Tessa. Even when you might think you can't, please just trust me." Dean stood and paced to the clearing at the edge of the forest where the grass sloped down to the foothills. "You coming?"

"I've been waiting all week for this." She rushed to catch up with him. "Time to show me what you can do." During their last sessions, they were focused on getting Dean back on his feet and up to speed with her gift. But she hadn't experienced his gift yet. She only knew what he'd told her that night at Amrita. His quirky little gift that told him when someone was honest and trustworthy. That night he'd said she was one of the most trustworthy people he'd ever met, but she wondered if he would say that same thing now.

"Your elemental gift is so sophisticated, Tessa. A vital gift this world needs right now. Mine is similar in some ways. Maybe even more than we realize." He crouched low to the ground, sinking his hands into the soil.

"Your gift. It brings you pleasure and pain, yes?"

"Embracing my power is one of the most freeing sensations I've ever known. I can't describe it."

"Mine is the same." He sifted the dark soil through his hands. "The pain comes when I am healing the man-made damage done to nature. I can feel the earth's suffering at our heedless abuse."

"It's the same for me too," Tessa whispered. Hearing him talk of his gift was like hearing herself. They were similar in so many substantial ways; it sometimes felt like they'd known each other all their lives. But at the same time, they were near strangers. She didn't really know a thing about him but she wanted to.

Dean slipped his hands into the loose soil, clenching his fists just under the surface.

Tessa gasped as new growth sprouted up all around them. Tiny saplings, bushes, grass, and flowers. Fresh seedlings peeked through the ground, reaching for the sunlight. Sweat beaded across his brow, but Dean dug his hands in deeper, the corded muscles of his arms standing out in sharp relief. Exotic flowers began to bud, and the most unusual saplings spread their dark ebony limbs.

Tessa watched in awe as the makings of a jungle sprouted at her feet and all across the hillside. Dean finally released a breath, his eyes flashing silver in the sunlight as he sat on the ground. He pulled his shaking hands from the rich soil. Taking a deep breath, he fought to reign in his power. She could see the toll it took on him. She'd experienced much the same with the use of her gift.

"That was amazing." She knelt beside him. "We are going to do so much good working in the jungles of South America. This growth is still very young. How long would it take you to grow an acre of rainforest?"

"Several weeks, with lots of rest in between."

"And revitalizing a forest that has been damaged?"

"Much more painful but also much faster."

"Dean, between your gift and mine, we could change the face of the world." Excitement bubbled up inside her. She was more eager than ever to get started.

He nodded, taking her hand in his. "We could. But that all depends on what Vivian Dyson has planned for us."

CHAPTER 8

"Nearly there," Ryan said absently. He didn't seem to be looking forward to visiting his family. But that was part of his job, escorting agents to their assignments. He would meet with Vivian first while Dean and Tess got settled in their new home.

Anticipation had her on the edge of her seat as they bumped along the winding road through the jungle along the *Tiputini* river. Vivian's base of operations was located in the *Cuya Beno* Reserve in the jungles of Columbia at the convergence of the *Tiputini* and *Conejo* rivers. The reserve was home to some of the most beautiful vegetation and fauna she'd ever seen. Few were allowed to step foot into the reserve, and she was one of them. She couldn't wait to finally be able to use her gift for something more than practice.

Tessa's mind was filled with grand ideas of how she would impress her new boss. She didn't have it in her to watch the way Dean seemed to retreat into himself the closer they got to their destination. Today was the day she'd waited for since the moment she joined Soma. She couldn't let anything or anyone ruin this experience for her. Not even Dean.

"What's your home like?" she asked Ryan.

"It's not my home. Mother and Father moved here just a few years ago. This is the first time I've been here." His jaw ticked with tension. Apparently, Ryan wasn't looking forward to this visit with his family. Probably because his brother, Michael, had gone missing along with Livia, Quinn, and Santi. There was no news of any of them. None that she was privy to.

"When we arrive, you will meet with Brecken, the head of Mother's staff. He will get you settled. You will answer to him while you're here." Ryan slowed the Jeep to a crawl along a particularly rough patch of road. "Here we are. Home sweet home." He turned onto a gravel road that led to a high, ornate gate. He roughly punched in a code, and the gates opened, revealing a paved drive. They soon left the confines of the jungle behind as the sky opened above them. The rolling, grassy hills seemed out of place at the center of the rainforest. Almost unnatural.

"This all used to be marshland," Ryan said, waving at the huge lawn. "It's been transformed to look like our home in rural Georgia, so Mother doesn't have to look at the 'god-forsaken' jungle all day. It took a horde of landscapers to make it happen."

With the *Tiputini* to the right, and the *Conejo* river to the left, Vivian's complex was like an island oasis, protected on all sides from any possible danger. It was breathtaking. Tessa's mouth dropped open at the sight of the exotic Mediterranean villa at the end of the drive. Pristine white against the green, green grass, the sprawling mansion was not quite what she had anticipated.

"It's lovely," she said in awe.

"Mother likes beautiful things." Ryan rolled to a stop under the covered portico where several very large Immortals patrolled the grounds around the house.

"Ryan, long time, no see." A burly, bearded man came to greet them.

"Brecken. Good to see you." The two men greeted each other in a big, back slapping man-hug. "Your mother's eagerly waiting your arrival."

"I'll just bet she is." Ryan took the steps up to the entrance two at a time.

"Sorry to hear about Michael," Brecken called at his retreating figure. "Let's have a drink before you leave."

"Better be quick., I'm out of here as soon as possible." Ryan's wave was the last Tessa saw of him. She frowned at the slam of the front door. No introductions. No goodbye. He just left them at the curb like baggage.

"This way." Brecken's smile vanished along with his cheery demeanor the instant Ryan left.

This was the man in charge of Vivian's staff? He wasn't much older than Dean.

"I'm Tessa. And this is my student, Dean," she said as she followed Brecken, rushing to keep up with his long stride.

"I know," Brecken said, continuing around to the back of the mansion in silence.

The big house held every possible luxury, she was sure, but the building tucked behind the mansion was utilitarian at best. Large and square, the facility occupied the rear of the complex behind the gardens, the massive pool, and luxurious pool house. Two stories set at a lower elevation than the main house ensured that Vivian would never have to look at the ugly building.

"This is where you will live. You'll each have a solitary dormitory with everything you could possibly need. Nothing fancy, but it's comfortable enough."

"Here? I expected we would have rooms in the house." Tessa frowned at the cold concrete entrance. She was used to nice things. She'd worked hard for her status, and she expected to keep it.

"Lady, you're lucky I don't put you in a tent in the jungle. Get inside. It's bloody hot out here." Brecken shoved her through the door.

The coolness of the interior was definitely a comfort

after the heat of the day, but this was not going well. Nothing about this was anything like she'd expected. Tessa always heard stories of the amazing places other agents got to live and work, and they always had the best accommodations. Something wasn't right here.

"Are there others here?" She stared at the concrete floors and long corridors branching off in every direction.

"None that you need to concern yourself with. You will be isolated during your training."

Tessa nodded. "We understand." She wanted to protest his mention of training. She'd had enough training to last her a lifetime. She was ready to take action. But she thought better of voicing her concerns.

"I will be your immediate supervisor and trainer. You will follow my rules, and we'll get along just fine. You two will train together in the gym for a few hours each morning. That is all the time you will get with your student, so make it count."

"Yes, sir," Tessa said, grateful for Dean's silence. He walked behind her, glaring at everything, his hands shoved into his pockets. She was thrown by their odd arrival and ridiculously young supervisor. She'd trained circles around guys like him, and now she had to give him deference. It didn't make any sense.

"I expect you to be showered and dressed in your uniforms by ten a.m. each day, six days a week. You will train with me twelve hours a day, every day, for one month, and then you will be expected to perform your jobs on your own time."

"And what will those jobs be?" She was anxious to know.

"We will discuss that once I decide you're ready. I suggest you take tonight to get settled and rested."

"Who should we ask if we need anything?" Tessa assumed there was some sort of resident concierge to take care of such things.

"You will only have contact with me. If you need something, ask me after training each evening. Your rooms have been fully stocked. I expect you will not need anything, so don't annoy me with useless requests."

"Yes, sir."

"You will share a joint suite with a common area between." Brecken guided them down a long, stark hallway to their adjoining rooms.

"Chatty girl, you're in here." He opened the door to a tiny closet of a room. A twin bed occupied the rear wall of the windowless room. A desk and a dresser took up the remaining space. Everything was white. Even the quilt on the bed.

"Looks fine," Tessa managed to say. The room was depressing. By taking such a huge step forward in her career, she'd somehow taken a huge step down in her accommodations. She tentatively opened the door to the common area, hoping for a much larger shared space. What she found was a narrow walkway between her room and Dean's. On one side was a tiny bathroom they would have to share. On the other was a small kitchenette with a microwave, mini refrigerator, and the tiniest oven she'd ever seen. "Is there a cafeteria? Or a kitchen for meals?"

"You're looking at it. I hope you can cook. Your diet will consist of beans, rice, lean chicken, fresh fruits, and vegetables. Everything you can prepare here." Tessa took another look at the kitchenette, her stomach sinking down to her toes. *What is going on here?*

Dean snorted his reply and stepped into his room, a mirror image of hers. They would be living in close quarters indeed.

"Not so chatty, that one." Brecken nodded at Dean. "That's good. Keep it up. Uniforms are in the closet. You'll be responsible for your own laundry." He gestured to the curtained area beside the bathroom.

Tess peeked into the closet to see five sets of uniforms each. Hers were black and teal. Dean's were black and gray. A micro washer/dryer rested at the bottom of the closet. It was one of those tiny units that hooked to the sink with a hose and would wash and dry in one go.

"How do you distinguish rank here?" she asked, looking at the strange emblems on the uniform sleeves.

"Color. Red is the highest rank in the complex. That's all you need to know."

She noted his jeans and collared shirt were not just street clothes. The piping along his shirt was red, and his sleeve was adorned with half a dozen symbols marking his rank. He was in charge of everything, so he was the person she needed to impress the most.

How in the world did he get to be head of Vivian's staff?

"When will we meet with Vivian?" She had a lot of questions for her new employer.

"Never."

Tess couldn't stand the heat and humidity of the jungle.

"Keep up," Brecken shouted over his shoulder.

Tess rushed along the narrow path to catch up. This was Brecken's favorite game. Torturing Tessa. Their marathon training sessions kept her on the brink of exhaustion. Every night she collapsed into her tiny bed, too tired to keep her eyes open any longer. She'd never slept so much in her life.

"Last day of training. Time to show me what you're made of, chatty-girl. Your student's showing you up ... again."

Brecken and Dean raced up the path to the cliff. Dean, indeed, showed her up. Quite often. His training had prepared him for this. Hers, not so much. She'd always focused more on the use of her gifts than physical training. Her days had always been filled with sparring and honing her environmental gift, not racing up mountains and diving off cliffs to swim in the river. That kind of training was for those with lesser gifts. This wasn't the best use of her skills.

Tessa trudged up the steep incline, panting and sweating, lifting her limp hair out of her eyes. For nearly a month, she'd struggled to find her place here. Not the first impression she'd dreamed of making. But somehow, Dean seemed to flourish while she faltered.

Today was the day she'd finally find out why she was really here. Today was the last day of their month-long torture with Brecken. Tomorrow, the real work would begin, and that was where Tessa intended to shine.

With that thought in mind, she picked up her pace, charging toward the cliff's edge. She hated this part. The free-fall into the white water below, praying she wouldn't dash her head against the rocks, or get caught up in the current of the waterfall like she had the first day. Brecken had to rescue her. That had been completely humiliating.

Leaping over the edge, arms and legs flailing like a moron, she crashed into the warm, churning waters where the rivers converged. Sometimes she wanted to keep sinking into its muddy depths. To swim into the jungle and never look back. But that would forfeit any chance she had of becoming the rising star she'd always anticipated being. That was a dream she would not give up so easily. Someday she'd look back on this and laugh at herself. That day was not today.

Wheezing and trembling, Tessa pulled herself onto the

sandy river bank where she collapsed. Meanwhile, Dean and Brecken were cracking open a few protein drinks, laughing like they'd just gone out for a simple morning jog.

The two got along far too well. The way Dean had acclimated himself to this new normal was odd in the extreme. It was like he woke up that second day, fully embracing this life. He had no expectations. No ambition. He just needed to hunker down and get through it.

She tried to take it one day at a time the way he did, but she had so much more riding on this. She *had* to make this a success.

"Last time, doll-face," Brecken said. "I won't make you jump off cliffs anymore." His laughter caught her by surprise.

"Thanks for that," she said dryly.

"I just needed to see what you two are made of. I have my answers now. Dean will roll with whatever you throw at him, never letting it show how much he hates it, while you will kill yourself to achieve whatever I ask of you. Both are great qualities. You work well together, and that's what we need."

It was the highest of praise coming from Brecken. Something had changed. Like the initial test was over and they'd passed.

"Go get cleaned up, and meet me in the gym in an hour."

Tessa raced through the forest back to the path leading to the complex. They had to cook, eat, and shower in one hour, and they had it down to a science. Tess hopped into the shower as soon as she reached their dorm. While she dressed, Dean set the rice and beans to boil and cut fresh fruits for their meal.

"I got it from here. Go grab a shower. We should have enough hot water left for a quick one." She slipped past him in the tiny kitchen. There was barely enough room for them to navigate the small space.

"You okay, Tessa?" Dean's hands rested on her shoulders to stop her furious activity.

"I'm fine. Just nervous about today." She took a breath, trying to make herself relax.

"You've got this." He tilted her chin up to meet his gaze.

"I've bungled this whole thing so far." She gave a humorless laugh.

"Hey, no one expects you to be perfect at everything. Well, no one but you." He smiled, tucking a strand of wet hair behind her ear. "Brecken's just been evaluating us."

"That's just great. He probably wonders why Soma ever bothered with me."

"Tessa." Dean rolled his eyes and pulled her close. "He's just been evaluating which one of us is the muscle and which one of us is the brains. After this last month, he knows you're the one with all the drive, and I'm the one who doesn't give a shit."

"I just ... I have to make a better impression today. Go get your shower. We can't be late."

"All right, but I get the hot shower next time." He folded

his long frame into the tiny bathroom and the even tinier shower.

Tess grabbed the chicken marinating in the fridge and set to work finishing their meal. She warmed homemade flour tortillas in the toaster-who knew Dean could bake? And she chopped peppers and onions for fajitas to go with their staple of beans and rice. Most days neither of them felt much like cooking, so they tended to opt for simple, bland meals. But she felt like celebrating today. It was a milestone. Today, things would start looking up. They had to.

Dean emerged from the bathroom with a pristine white towel draped around his slim hips. A sight she never tired of seeing. The Soma brand peeked out at her from the towel. She'd wondered why he decided to put the symbol right above his ass. When she'd asked him about it, he said it was because he'd told Ryan to kiss his ass when he'd asked where Dean wanted the brand.

"Smells good." He stepped behind her, placing his hands on her hips as he moved in the narrow space. Living in such close quarters, they'd quickly gotten over any initial awkwardness. The doors between them rarely closed anymore.

"I was in the mood for something with flavor." She leaned against him. When they were here in their home, they dropped all the professionalism at the door. In here they were friends. Friends who needed the comfort the other provided. The attraction between them was strong, but the timing and the place was all wrong. A touch here, an embrace there was as far as it ever went. But for Tessa it was enough.

"I'm starving." Dean filled his plate and stepped into his room to finish dressing. "Let me throw on some clothes and come join me."

Not for the first time, she wished they had a small table and a little more free time so they could enjoy a meal together. Tessa fixed her plate and made them both a glass of iced tea.

"I'll get the drinks, Tessa." He stepped back into the kitchen, dressed in his black and gray uniform.

She followed him into the room and perched on the edge of his bed.

"Why do you always call me Tessa?" She shoveled a bite of fajita into her mouth as fast as she could chew. They had to meet Brecken in twenty minutes, and she still had to dry her hair.

"That's your name." Dean sat at his desk, scarfing his food down with a gulp of tea.

"Most people call me Tess."

"I like Tessa. It's a beautiful name." He winked. "And I'm not most people. At least I don't want to be most people with you."

Tessa swallowed her chicken and peppers over the lump in her throat.

"Another time and place..." She shrugged.

"Another time and place," Dean echoed.

"This is so nerve-wracking." Tessa smiled as they walked down the long corridor to the gym after their mad dash through lunch. She twisted her hands together. "I'm so excited and terrified at the same time."

"I expect more of the same," Dean grunted his reply.

"Come on, this will be good for us."

"For your sake, I hope it is." He managed a hesitant smile.

"Why do you say that?"

"You've worked so hard for this. I just hope it's not a disappointment."

"Don't be so negative, Dean. This is a *good* thing. The torture is behind us."

"Exercise is not torture, Tessa." He rolled his eyes, opening the door to the gymnasium. It was even more state of the art than the gym at Soma, and that was saying something.

"Gather around, guys," Brecken called from his office at the back of the gym.

Tessa and Dean took the plush seats opposite his desk. It was the first time in a month she'd sat in an actual comfortable chair. Her body melted into the soft fabric. She'd give anything to have a chair like this in her room. Maybe she was in a position now where she could ask for one.

"Before I take you on a tour of the facilities where you'll be working, let's talk about the perks you've earned."

"Perks?" Dean asked.

"You've both worked hard, and we like to reward hard work to our loyal staff. From this day forward, you are both on equal footing. You will both take the yellow uniform to indicate your status as trained and skilled staff members. You will continue to work with me, exclusively for one year. At that time, you will be re-evaluated."

"A year?" Tessa gasped. Most Soma agents worked their first assignments on much shorter terms before they moved on to their next one. She hadn't anticipated being here that long. From all her years of training and preparing for this, having so many things catch her off guard made her uneasy.

"At a minimum, yes," Brecken replied. "As we speak, you're being moved to a larger suite with two bathrooms and a much larger common area. We want you to be comfortable. You'll also receive an extra fifteen minutes for lunch and dinner breaks."

Tessa could have fainted with relief.

"What's the catch?" Dean asked.

Tessa wanted to slap him. Showing anything but gratitude was the quickest way to get their privileges revoked. But she caught the telltale sign of his mistrust. If Dean sensed something wasn't on a level, she'd learned to be wary.

"No catch. Just keep doing what you've been doing, and you'll be on easy street from here on out. After three months if we are pleased with your work ethic, you'll be granted more privileges. And eventually, you will earn the freedom to come and go as you please during your off time, of which you will receive more."

"Sounds amazing, thank you," Tessa said before Dean could make things worse. If Brecken wasn't being completely honest, then they would figure that out soon enough. There was no need to piss him off now when he was handing out rewards.

"And what will we be doing?" Dean asked.

"Come with me." Brecken stood. "You will report to me each morning at nine, after your personal time in the gym, of course. We expect you to be putting in at least four hours of training every day, with Sundays off. You will meet me here." Brecken stopped at a pair of double doors that had always been locked before but stood open now.

"Where are we going?" Tessa peered past him at the enormous garage behind him.

"Deep into the jungle. Hop in. We have a hour drive there and back."

Tessa and Dean silently piled into the jeep. Dean looked almost sick, while Tessa felt like something was finally going right. The drive was slow going along the treacherous roads into the rainforest, but she anticipated they would be traveling through this kind of terrain a lot over the coming year.

Tessa expected to see polluted wetlands or stagnant pools of water not fit for drinking that she would need to fix. She did not expect to find an endless sea of water drums arranged in neat rows nestled into the midst of the jungle as far as she could see.

"What is this?"

"Stockpiled water for your use. Ever since we knew you were coming, we've been planning for this."

"But this is clean water. What do you need me for?" Tessa didn't even know what to think of this latest development.

"You've been training for this for years, Tess."

"I've been preparing to restore polluted ecosystems to their natural state. I've been training for a year to make the foulest waters safe to drink."

"And you've been learning to separate the particulates and elements found in water, leaving behind only what you want to leave. We've been told you are the best at this particular kind of gift."

"That is true, but I don't see how that will be put into practice here."

"Electrolysis, Tessa," Dean said softly.

"Exactly," Brecken said.

"No." Tessa shook her head stubbornly. "That is not the best use of my gift."

"That is not for you to decide," Brecken said irritably. "The question here is, can you do it?"

"Theoretically, yes, but why would you need that much hydrogen?" She flung her hand in the direction of thousands of gallons of perfectly drinkable water.

"Fuel cell energy," Dean offered. "Cheap, clean energy no one else could manage on this scale without you."

"Renewable energy," Brecken added. "And with the help of the very talented Tessa St. James, cheaper than cheap. No one else bothers with electrolysis on a large scale because it takes more energy to produce pure hydrogen than that hydrogen yields. But with you, we get the energy without all the hassle."

"You have no idea what you're asking." Tessa felt sick. She couldn't do this. She'd have to go home a complete failure.

"Tell me this isn't going to be a problem, Tessa. We've gone to a lot of trouble to bring you here."

"I-you realize how difficult this will be? How exhausting ... and painful it will be for me to do this? Removing toxins from water is easy enough because they don't belong. But even that can make me terribly ill, depending on what's in the water. Removing everything so that the only thing left behind is pure hydrogen ... it will be like ripping myself apart to get through a gallon."

"Well, this is the only thing required of you. You'll have twelve to sixteen hours each day. You may rest when you need it. But we expect a certain output, and we expect that output to increase over time."

"It will take me a year to get through one or two of these drums."

"That's not acceptable. We are aiming for ten thousand gallons of water to be converted to pure, liquid hydrogen this year. You will work in the lab daily until you meet your quota."

"I-I'll do my best." Tessa wanted to cry. She'd always seen her gift as a beautiful thing she could give to the world. To take her completely out of nature, putting her into a clinical lab, it would be torture. A perverse use of her gift. What had Soma committed her to?

"Your best is all we expect of you."

Tessa's mind reeled with disappointment. They wanted cheap, clean energy with an endless supply only she could provide. They would make millions off her back, through her blood, sweat, and tears.

A shot of cold, stark reality rippled through her. How long would this go on?

"Dean, you have such a remarkable gift. I've never seen anything quite like it." Brecken clapped him on the back as they walked through the maze of water drums, each containing one thousand gallons of water Tessa would have to practically kill herself to convert to hydrogen. Heartbroken, Tessa struggled to put one foot in front of the other.

"And what amazing use of my gift have you all cooked up for me?" The fury in Dean's voice was clear. He was not amused by the way things had gone for Tessa.

He cast a concerned glance in her direction. He seemed

to recognize how completely crushed she was over this assignment.

"We just found out about you, so we aren't as prepared, but luckily you don't need much to work with."

As they walked along a narrow pathway beyond the field of water drums, Tessa's heart dropped into her stomach at the sight of such ruin. Huge trees lay stacked in neat rows of logs. The ground looked like a minefield where ancient root systems had been ripped from the soil.

The pain of her gift took her breath away. Dean stumbled to a halt, his eyes narrowing with anger. His fists clenched tightly at his sides. If his gift worked anything like Tessa's, this needless destruction caused him the same physical pain she was experiencing.

"Priceless exotic woods grow in this rainforest. Species that don't grow in abundance anywhere else on earth. It's illegal to cut them down," Brecken explained.

"Then why have you?" Tessa demanded. It was unethical and beyond reprehensible that they would do this.

"Because they want me to grow it back, so they can do this again and again. And again."

"Correct," Brecken said. "We will present the exotic woods as a newly discovered renewable resource previously hidden in the depths of the South American jungles. Valkyrie Enterprises will have a corner on the exotic woods market, not to mention the rare flowers and anything else you manage to grow for us."

"It hurts him," Tessa said, anger vibrating in her voice.

"The use of his gift in this way ... for both of us ... it goes against nature. Our gifts are environmental, and you're asking us to rape the world of its resources for money!"

"So you do get it," Brecken said coldly. "Anything less than what we've asked of you is unacceptable, and there will be punishments. If you cooperate and get on board, you will be rewarded. Any stress your job requires of you will be treated immediately ... if your performance meets expectations. You can live like royalty here. Or we can do this the hard way. It's entirely up to you."

Chapter 10

"How do you do it, Dean?" Tessa asked. "How do you take it all in stride the way you do?"

He shrugged, easing back into his ridiculous leather recliner in their living room. She'd asked for a comfortable armchair; he'd asked for the most hideous, leather Barcalounger they could find.

"It's not like we really have a choice, Tessa." He pulled her down beside him.

Tessa lay her head on his chest, begrudgingly admitting the chair was insanely comfortable.

"I need to speak with Jayesh. This isn't right. We shouldn't be treated like ... like ... this." She couldn't even think of a word to describe the way they were being treated.

"Well, it's not like Brecken is going to let you borrow his phone anytime soon."

"It's exhausting, what they have us doing. What you go through every day." She looked up at him. "The stress on your gift. The pain it causes you when they tear down the forests you've created with your bare hands. It's unbearable to watch."

"I'm familiar with that particular torture." He stroked the length of her arms. "You work yourself to the bone every day. It kills me when I have to carry you out of that lab because you're in so much pain you can't walk. And yet you hit your quotas every time. That's why we get to enjoy our creature comforts here in the loft. This is our home, Tessa. When we're here, it's just us and nothing out there can touch us."

"You're right. We shouldn't even talk about what goes on out there. The loft needs to be our happy place." Brecken was true to his word. The day they found out about their jobs, they were moved to a two bedroom loft above the garage. They each had a spacious bedroom, with comfortable queen beds and their own bathrooms upstairs. And they shared the kitchen, dining, and living room downstairs. Even though they each had their own space now, they rarely spent their free time apart. They hadn't earned television privileges yet, so their waking nights were spent reading and resting in the peaceful quiet they only had when they were together.

"Hey, kids." Brecken let himself into the front foyer. He never knocked.

Tessa scrambled back to her own chair. It wouldn't do for anyone to see just how close they were.

"You both had much better production rates this month than you did last month and even the month before. Great job." He handed them each an iPad as a reward. "You are restricted to visiting two sites. Netflix and Primely. You can order just about anything you want within reason. Your monthly stipend is in your accounts. Go nuts."

Tessa stared at the screen with a frown after Brecken left. She tapped on the Primely app. The action was such a familiar part of her life at Soma. She cast a glance around the New York style loft, with the exposed brick walls and shiny, sleek surfaces. She'd never noticed it before, but there were a lot of similarities here to her life back at Soma. The way they were rewarded for a job well done. The ranking system. She glanced down at the yellow stripes on her shirt. She'd earned a few more accolades since she'd taken the yellow uniform. With each passing day, they cooperated just a little bit more, acclimating to the way of life here. They lived in luxurious accommodations with all the comforts they needed. A special thanks for how difficult and physically demanding their jobs were. Now they had almost everything they could desire at their fingertips. And every month they banked a nice salary, never having to spend a dime on living expenses. Tessa was able to send her mother a larger stipend that had allowed her to quit one of her jobs. Being able to do that for her mom had made much of this experience worth it. But what was all of this?

"Let's get one of those fancy coffee machines," Dean suggested.

Tessa let out a strangled shriek as she threw the iPad across the room, watching it shatter against the wall.

"How could I have been so blind?" She had the word for it now: slave. Tessa St. James was a slave. She'd been a slave her whole life and never realized it until this very moment. "I'm such an idiot." She gripped the edges of her chair, fighting the urge to throw it. All her life she'd done what was asked of her as those she trusted trained her to be an arrogant fool, too stupid to see the shiny things they threw at her were nothing but treats you'd give a dog for good behavior.

Dean knelt in front of her, prying her hands from the armrests. "I take it you get it now?"

She nodded as tears of frustration streaked down her face. She moaned like a wounded animal, fighting to take a breath. Tessa met his cold gaze and saw the hate in his eyes. Not for her, but for what had been done to them. She touched his face where he'd been injured upon his arrival at Soma. He hadn't joined. He wasn't a recruit. They'd taken him by force. Ripped him from his family. And he'd protected her from that knowledge.

Her gaze hardened as she gripped his hands. "How much do you think Soma made when they sold us to Vivian?"

"So that's why you've been so agreeable since we got here?" Tessa shook her head as they walked across the grassy hills behind the loft. Dean wasn't sure it was safe for them to talk freely in their home. They only spoke of their escape when they were certain they were alone. In the weeks since Tessa finally saw the truth, they'd continued to perform well in their jobs. As they earned more privileges, Brecken's watchful eye began to relax, and they had more free time.

"Make your enemy feel like they've conquered you, and they'll grow complacent, thinking they have the upper hand."

"Giving us the time to make our plans. I want to leave now, Dean." She gazed into the rainforest, thinking they could conquer whatever was out there as long as they stayed together.

"We have to take this slow. Everyone here needs to believe we are satisfied with the way things are. Let them think they've bought us with the nice apartment, money, and frivolous things. We bide our time, get them to trust us. Let Brecken think of us as friends. We earn the right to come and go as we please. And then one day, we walk out of here and never come back."

"They'll have ways of tracking us," Tessa said. She had no illusions about her status at Soma now. She had been fooled by all the praise and promises of a great life with Soma at her back. Growing up in a world where she was rewarded for doing what she was told and excelling at every task set before her-it didn't set her apart from the rest. Soma stroked her ego, letting her and her poor mother believe she was truly something special. That she was better than others. Tessa wasn't special. She was just a gullible child who'd turned into a well-trained slave, and sacrificed her life with her mother for nothing.

"We'll deal with that when the time comes. The plan now is to get them to trust us enough to give us all the freedoms we can earn. In time, we'll make our move."

"Patience? I've never had much of that."

"We will get our lives back, Tessa."

"And then I will dedicate the rest of mine to ending Soma."

CHAPTER 11

SEVERAL YEARS LATER

"Get up, lazy girl." Dean jumped onto the bed they shared in the little cottage they'd earned more than a year ago. It was Tessa's happy place. When they were in their home, everything else paled in comparison to the life they had under this roof. "It's Sunday, Tessa."

"Our day." She sat up, her messy blond hair falling around her shoulders.

"Ready for a hike?" He leaned in for a kiss. "Or will it be another Sunday spent in bed? Your choice."

"A hike to our valley?"

"Of course."

"Meet you out front in twenty minutes." She jumped out of the bed and scrambled to find her hiking clothes.

Thanks to Brecken, they had a little piece of land that was all theirs. A place to heal the wounds inflicted by the work they did for Valkyrie enterprises. Six months into their assignment, both Tess and Dean had grown dangerously ill. Fletcher Dyson actually came to visit them. He immediately recognized the source of their bad health. The work they were forced to do was such a perverse use of their gifts that they were suffering the consequences. It was Brecken's idea to give them the valley. A place where they could go to use their gifts in their own ways-how they were meant to be used. Fletcher made it happen, despite his wife's vehement disapproval. Vivian never deigned to visit them, but allowed this one small kindness because it improved her bottom line.

The valley was theirs, and it gave them an outlet to ease their physical pain. As a result, Dean and Tess grew healthy again.

"I wish we could move our little house there," Tess said as she joined Dean on their front porch. Together, they set off across the grassy lawn to the trail leading into the jungle. It was a short hike to their valley.

When they'd first arrived, the valley was nothing more than a swamp. Vivian gave them her most useless track of land, and they'd turned it into a paradise.

Tessa used her gift in ways she'd never dreamed of to restore the marshy land to a pristine lake of clear, fresh water with a beautiful waterfall. Dean turned the surrounding land into a lovely meadow, bordered by a lush forest with the most exotic species of flowers. Some she was certain no one had ever seen before.

"Are you happy here, Tessa?" Dean asked when they arrived on the hillside overlooking their valley. It was something he asked often when they were here. Sometimes the answer was no. She'd never be truly happy without her freedom.

"Today, I am happy." She reached up on tiptoes to kiss the most important person in her world. The thought of being here alone terrified her. She thanked Jayesh everyday for sending Dean with her. She often wondered if he did it on purpose to give her a chance of surviving this mess.

"I want you to be happy every day." Dean sat on the grassy slope, pulling her down beside him.

"Sometimes I think I could be happy with this life. It can't last forever. And there are times when it's not so bad. We're treated well. We have each other. It should be enough."

"But it's not." He sighed. "It's not enough for either of us."

"Not when I think of all the kids Soma has exploited in the name of the almighty dollar. One of these days, we're going to make it out of here. And when we do, I'm going after Soma."

"I don't know, maybe we should try leaving through the jungle," he said.

They'd talked about it often. The day they arrived, Tessa had thought the way the rivers wrapped around the complex made it a beautiful oasis tucked into the jungle. Now, she realized it was a prison. There were things out there she'd never anticipated. The only way out of this place was through the front gate.

"We can't risk it. I don't think Brecken would really hurt us, but his barrier is so dangerous." Just beyond the rivers lay a slice of the Dreamworld-their prison walls. If Tess and Dean ventured too far beyond the rivers, they would wander into the Dreamworld where they might be lost forever. Knowing so little about it, they had never felt confident enough to try it. They were stuck.

Tessa had a hard time wrapping her mind around it when she'd first learned of it. Brecken was a dreamwalker. A talented one, which explained why he had become head of Vivian's staff at such a young age. The Dreamworld was an ancient place, and he was the first true dreamwalker born in many centuries. The way he spoke of it, he was a king there, and the older walkers feared him.

"He might be willing to help us," Dean said. Over the years they'd all become friends, but they never forgot their roles.

"He is too distracted these days. Something's happening in the dreamworld he doesn't like. I heard him talking about it with someone on the phone the other day. It sounds almost like there is a war brewing there."

"Another reason we shouldn't risk it." Dean sighed.

Despite the friendship they now shared, Brecken had learned quickly that the best way to punish them was to split them up. They now had the freedom to come and go as they pleased. They could even leave the complex with Brecken as an escort and visit the Valkyrie Enterprise holdings across the globe. But they could never go together. If Dean left, Tessa had to stay behind. And Brecken knew there was no way either of them would ever leave without the other.

"Let's not talk about anything depressing today. This is our day." Tessa stood and held out her hand. "Let's go swimming."

"Don't shoot. I know I'm not allowed in the love valley," Brecken called as he jogged down the path to join them.

"What's up?" Dean stood to greet their boss.

"I'm sorry to interrupt on your day off. I know this place is sacred ground, but you need to come with me. Vivian is waiting for you. And she's mad as hell."

"Vivian? What could she want after all this time?" Tessa frowned. She'd never laid eyes on the woman.

"I don't know, but she's not happy. We better run," Brecken said.

"Let's go." Dean took off down the path back to the main house. Neither of them had ever stepped a foot inside the mansion before today.

"Through here," Brecken said. They followed him through the rear servant's entrance and down the cool marble hallway.

"Mrs. Dyson?" Brecken knocked on her office door.

"Bring them in."

Tessa trembled as she followed Dean into the room.

Someone else was here with Vivian. Someone she knew. She choked on the hope rising in her chest, smashing it back down. If this place had taught her anything, it was to not let hope take root in her mind. It only caused her pain.

"Jayesh?" she managed to get his name out when she saw him sitting opposite Vivian.

"Dean, Tessa." Jayesh nodded at each of them. "Thank you for coming."

"What can we do for you?" Dean asked politely. He didn't seem as confused as she did. He seemed relieved. Like he'd been waiting for this day for a long, long time.

What has he kept from me?

"Soma has need of you. Vivian has graciously agreed to let you come home for a short while."

"A very short while. And this is their home," she said sharply. "Don't forget that small detail, Jayesh. I paid a fortune for these two."

"Yes, you did. And we do respect that they are essentially your property, Vivian, but we do include a recall clause in all of our contracts. If Soma ever has need of a particular gift, or gifts, the individual is recalled to Sterling Tower. They will be returned to you as soon as possible."

"I'd still prefer to send Brecken with them. To monitor my assets."

"I'm afraid that is against the rules you agreed upon when you purchased them. I have a copy of the contract here."

Tessa was furious, listening to them speak so bluntly

about them. As if they were pieces of meat one might buy at the grocery store.

"Then by all means go, so you can get them back to me. Every day they are gone, we lose money. A lot of money."

"You will be compensated as you deserve. I promise." Jayesh smiled.

"Shall we ... go pack?" Tessa asked, not believing what was happening.

"No. You'll have everything you need when we arrive back in Atlanta."

"We're leaving now?" She took a tentative step toward the door, clutching Dean's hand. She was eager to go as quickly as possible but after all this time, she didn't trust that they wouldn't be separated.

Jayesh nodded and stood to escort them from their prison.

Bewildered, Tessa followed as they walked right out of the front door and slid into the backseat of Jayesh's black SUV.

The driver's side door slammed shut, and they were rolling down the driveway. Really fast.

"We need to get through those gates before she has a chance to compare that fake contract to the original," Dean said, looking over his shoulder.

"What?" Tessa glanced between Dean and Jayesh.

"Let's get out of sight of the house first," Jayesh muttered. "I have a helicopter waiting nearby. We'll be out of here faster than she'll react."

"What's going on?" Tess demanded. "Dean, what do you know?"

"We're going home, Tessa." He clasped her hands, shaking with relief.

"I don't understand. You lied to me? All this time?"

"Only because you suck at lying," he swore. "I wanted to tell you, but we couldn't risk it."

"I couldn't get out of sending you here, Tess," Jayesh said as he picked up speed, racing through the gate that stood wide open for them. "The best I could do was send Dean with you, so you wouldn't be alone through all of this. It's the only thing I could do for you."

"To be fair, he's a few years later picking us up than we planned," Dean said.

"I'm so sorry. A lot has happened while you've been here. This is the first chance I've had to come get you. We need you both."

"I won't go back to Soma," Tessa insisted.

"I don't work for Soma anymore," Jayesh said. "And neither do you."

"We don't have to go back?" Tessa gasped as the weight of what he was saying hit her.

"You never have to go back."

"We're finally free, Tessa" Dean whispered.

Epilogue

"What's in Cleveland?" Tessa asked. The journey from South America to Cleveland had overwhelmed her. So much had happened in such a whirlwind of chaos, she still had more questions than answers. Like who was the nice man in dreadlocks Dean seemed to know so well? His name was George. He'd flown them out of Vivian's reach in the most confusing helicopter ride of her life. He'd also done something to their Soma brands. Said it would fade in time, but once Ryan learned of their escape, he would probably attempt to call them back. George said that might hurt a bit.

He hadn't lied about that.

"My family is here," Dean said.

"We're going to meet with some friends, and then you'll have all your answers," Jayesh said. "I promise."

Tessa followed them from the airport where a driver met

them at the curb. He was quiet in the extreme. Tall and fair like a Viking right out of the history books.

"Uncle Liam." Dean clapped him on the shoulder. "It's good to see you." He took the seat right behind his uncle. "This is my girlfriend, Tessa."

"Good to meet you, Tessa. We're glad to have you both back. We've missed you, Dean. Your mother hasn't been the same without you."

"Did you have to nail Sasha to the floor to keep her home?" Jayesh asked, slipping into the seat beside Dean while George took the front seat with Liam.

"I had to let her come to the meeting to get her to stay put. She doesn't like it when you leave," Liam said.

"Well, I haven't given her much cause to trust me when I say I'm coming back," Jayesh said.

"You're still too old for my niece." Liam pulled away from the curb.

"I agree. We've talked about that, Liam."

"Just so you remember."

"Sasha is your cousin from Amrita?" Tessa whispered.

"Yeah, she is my dad's brother's daughter. His other brother." He nodded at Liam. "Let's just say the family tree is quite large but you'll get it in time."

"And what is this meeting all about?" she asked.

"We're about to find out." Dean nodded as they pulled into a parking lot in front of a bar not too far from the airport.

"Is there a reason we're meeting in such a seedy dive?" she asked.

"Yes," Liam said, holding the door open for her. "This is my bar."

"Oh." Tessa flushed. "I'm sorry. It's ... nice."

"It's nicer inside." He cracked a smile. "And it's safe to talk here. Come on in. The others are waiting."

Tessa followed the big man into a really crappy one room bar with just a few patrons. All of them were Immortal. None of them looked very above board.

"Through to the back," Dean whispered. "This is just a front."

"Oh." Tessa's eyes rounded as they stepped through a doorway into the back hall of the bar where the restrooms were.

"This way." Liam punched a code into a locked door and stepped through. It was like walking through the brick wall at the Leaky Cauldron into Diagon Alley. Where the front room was dirty and dingy, the back room was elegant and polished. Sleek, black marble floors were polished to a shine at her feet. The floor to ceiling glass windows faced the river with a large oak conference table occupying the center of the room.

The mood was tense. This was a war room, and Tessa recognized more than one person she never expected to see again.

"Livia?" Tessa found her voice as she took a step toward the woman who had ruined her life.

"That's far enough." Liam stepped in front of her. "My wife is not the person you remember."

"Your *wife*?"

"Much has happened since we last saw each other." Livia came to stand beside her Complement. "I don't deserve it, but I hope you will give me a chance. As trapped as you've been for most of your life, I have been as well. Soma was my prison, too."

"We have a lot to discuss and not a lot of time to do it. Please everyone, take your seats." Tessa recognized the redhead as Dean's powerful friend from that night at Amrita. She also recognized Quinn and Santi with Sasha and Jayesh standing beside them. She was thrilled to see James again and wondered if Lennox was with Dean's family now. A few others she didn't recognize but suspected they were part of Dean's inner circle.

For some inexplicable reason, everyone in this room seemed to defer to the young redhead and the man at her side. There was something odd about the bond between them. They weren't Complements, but they were ... something more. Something she'd never seen before.

"My name is Allie Carmichael, and this is my Syntrophos, Darius McBrien." She gestured at the man standing sentinel at her side. Tessa had no idea what a Syntrophos was, but the word rang with some kind of ancient power she would never understand. These two were something truly special. "Most of you know me. Some of you know how much I've battled accepting this Immortal life and my position in it. I never wanted this ... any of it. But our world is changing, and our generation is suffering. My maternal grandmother, Queen Alísun, the last queen of Indriell, has named me her heir. A position I've resisted for years, but have finally learned to accept."

She's a royal? Tessa glanced at Dean beside her. He didn't seem surprised. The hair was a dead giveaway that the girl had a strong connection to Indriell, but a direct line to the last queen? It couldn't be possible.

"I am the second natural daughter of Kassandre and Ashar. My mother, Kassandre, was the natural daughter of Queen Alísun. My elder sister is Livia. She was once my enemy and is now my strength and my ally. Together, we are going after Soma, and we are asking you all to join us."

Allie took her seat at the head of the table. "Soma isn't the only entity using and abusing our generation, but they are the worst, claiming to be something we all desperately need in a guise to lure us in, only to be sold into slavery. It has to end.

"Livia and I are going to return to Soma, and then we are going to work to bring it down from the inside and build it back up into the institution it claims to be. And then we're going after the others. Most of you have already agreed to help. But we still need you, Tessa. And Dean. You both have a unique experience with the enemy. Others will look to you for the truth. Tessa? Are you with us?"

For so long, she had trusted blindly, and then her whole world crashed down around her. Part of Tessa wanted to walk away from it all. To go find some small corner of the world where she and Dean could be happy together. They'd earned it. But a much larger part of her knew she could never leave her generation and the next to be used as she had.

"I'm in." She nodded firmly, not sure if she was supposed to bow to the First Princess of Indriell. She got the impression Allie wouldn't care for that at all. The only thing that mattered to Tessa now was going after Soma. If Allie and her people were leading the charge, Tessa was sure as hell going to do her part to bring down the institution that raised her. Soma would never destroy another child's life again.

Allie let out the breath she'd been holding. "Good because someone I love is in trouble and I need your help. All of you."

What will happen next for Allie and her friends?

Read on to find out in

Heir: Immortals of Indriell Book 4

DON'T FORGET YOUR FREE BOOK

In Assignment, find out what happens when Tessa St. James receives her first Assignment as a Soma Agent. And then download your FREE copy of SCHOLAR and discover everything there is to know about the Immortals of Indriell.

Visit http://bit.ly/SCHOLARoffer to download now!

Also by Melissa A. Craven

Immortals of Indriell Series:

Emerge (Book 1) | Catalyst (An Immortals of Indriell Short Story) | Edge (Book 0) | Judgment (Book 2) | Scholar (Series Companion Novel) | Volunteer (An Immortals of Indriell Short Story) | Captive (Book 3) | Assignment: An Immortals of Indriell Novella | Heir (Book 4) | Betrayal (Book 5) | Runaway (Book 6) | Proving (Book 7)

Queens of the Fae Series

Fae's Deception (Book 1)

Fae's Defiance (Book 2)

Fae's Destruction (Book 3)

Crimes of the Fae Series

Fae's Prisoner (Book 1)

Fae's Power (Book 2)

Fae's Promise (Book 3)

About Melissa A. Craven

Melissa A. Craven (the "A" stands for Ann—in case you were wondering) writes Young Adult Fantasy with crossover appeal to other genres and audiences of all ages. She believes in stories that make you think and she loves twisty plots, and playing with foreshadowing, leaving clues and hints for the careful reader. She draws inspiration from her background in architecture and interior design to help her with the small details in world building and scene settings. Melissa is also the indie manager and a staff reviewer at YABooksCentral.com. You can follow her reviews and her contributions to the YABC blog at the link below. And if you love Sweet Romance and Contemporary Fiction, you can find Melissa's books in those genres under her pen name, Ann Maree Craven.

Join Melissa's Underground on Facebook

facebook.com/MelissaACravenAuthor

twitter.com/melissaacraven

instagram.com/melissaacraven

bookbub.com/authors/melissa-a-craven

www.ingramcontent.com/pod-product-compliance
Lightning Source LLC
Chambersburg PA
CBHW030532310726
48979CB00010B/1887/J

* 9 7 8 1 9 7 0 0 5 2 1 4 5 *